HER HOLINESS
THE POPE

George Campbell Cunningham

British Library Cataloguing in Publication Data:
a catalogue record for this publication
is available from the British Library

© George Campbell Cunningham 2020

The right of George Campbell Cunningham to be identified as the
author of this work has been asserted by him in accordance with
the Copyright, Designs and Patents Act 1988

ISBN: 978-1-912052-58-5

Typeset in 11.5pt Minion Pro at Haddington, Scotland

Printed by West Port Print & Design, St Andrews

Cover design by Tom Campbell Cunningham

CONTENTS

Preface

The following short stories are an eclectic mix; some are thought-provoking, such as 'Her Holiness the Pope' while others are historical events seen through the eyes of people who I believe were there, such as 'For the Love of Mary'. These two in particular may seem slightly controversial but if they stimulate discussion then I have achieved something. On the other hand several have twists in the tale that aim to amuse such as 'The Pram, the Piglet and Maggie the Maid'. 'Goodbye, Mr Fogget' may also fall into this category as it is an out-of-body experience. However, some are just simply amusing; see 'The Battle o' the Bunnet' or 'The Rise and Fall of Wilberforce Clutterbarn'.

Several of these tales have sprung from observations or snatches of conversation that became the springboard for me to develop into stories. Also from dredging through my memory bank for interesting events from my youth that might lend themselves to be developed: 'The Ritual and the Laddie' is one such.

Dedication and Acknowledgments

Thanks to my wife Yvonne Cunningham, whose patience with my inability to untangle computer problems was essential. I'd also like to thank the poet Jock Stein for his invaluable advice, as well as my fellow Tyne and Esk Writers who have been my inspiration over the past decade.

HER HOLINESS THE POPE

An air of consternation was hanging over the Vatican, for the Pope was angry, really angry. 'Where did this ridiculous story come from?' he shouted. 'It must be stopped at all costs.' The Prefect of the Papal Household remained silent for a moment as he studied the floor. He was unused to outbursts of this nature. 'It cannot be true, Holiness,' he said, 'it is simply no more than malicious gossip.'

'But,' said the Pope, 'if it gains currency, it will cause a shiver to pass through the church and the enemies of our faith will tear us apart. Have you considered the consequences if this is leaked to the world's media?'

The Director of the Holy See press office coughed nervously. 'No media have contacted us to verify the claim,' he said, 'and, of course, we would deny it.' Silence followed.

Suddenly a note of hope attached to the Pope's voice. 'It is only a rumour, is it not? I mean no one will take it seriously, will they? Surely it can be left to die naturally. We've heard silly claims like this before.'

The Prefect sucked long and hard through his teeth. 'What you say is true, Holiness. But this story – I mean it is no more than gossip – has come from our Apostolic Nuncio and Ambassador Extraordinary to the European Union. I have quizzed him thoroughly and he tells me the whisper came from a very senior source in the United Kingdom . . .'

The Pope interrupted him, 'So that is it, it is no more than gossip. So, can we relax and let the matter wither as the grape will wither on the vine?' The director of the Holy See press office cleared his throat. 'The trouble,' he said 'will be if this well-placed source happens to mention it to the media. Because of his position he will be taken seriously.'

'Yes, yes,' said the Prefect, 'but if we deny it, laugh it off, then surely no newspaper, however outrageous its intent, will print it.' The Director was more sceptical. 'Nowadays the media show no respect for any organisation or person. That is the unfortunate truth and I fear if this rumour were to gain credence it would certainly make front pages worldwide.' 'In that case we must alert our Cardinals across the world to be sure to deny this rumour,' said the Prefect.

'No,' said the Pope loudly. 'Before we do anything, we must pray. The divine hand will guide us so we must seek His blessing. If His church is to be rocked by scandal, it will simply be to test our strength.'

So, in the privacy of his tiny chapel, deep in the Apostolic Palace, within the secure walls of Vatican City, the Pope knelt, but before he brought his hands together in prayer he allowed himself a moment of reflection. His gender reassignment had been so many years ago, when as a teenager he had the dilemma of being a young woman but also called by the same power to be a priest in the Catholic church. And he had always thought of himself as a man – but how damning it would be for him and the church if it was ever found out that the Pope had been born a woman.

FOR THE LOVE OF MARY

I am Judas Iscariot, friend of Jesus and one of the Twelve Disciples:

I have been with Jesus for a long time and he often asks my advice; we are good friends. I am more educated than most of the disciples and particularly the illiterate fishermen from Galilee. Also among us is Mary Magdalene a bright and beautiful woman and I am in love with her – but so is Jesus and that is causing tensions. The situation requires to be resolved. I have a plan.

I am Andrew, the First Chosen:

I'm worried about Jesus and I ask some of my more trustworthy fellow disciples if they share my concern. But I counsel them to stay silent on what we discus as I do not want Jesus to think we are conspiring against him and I do not want Mary to start interfering. I have not asked Judas to be with us as I am concerned he also may be part of the problem. So I ask those present, 'Friends, what can we do?'

My brother Simon Peter agrees there is unwanted tension and says there is no doubt in his mind that Jesus is, to put it mildly, unwell. He also says that others might suggest Jesus is off his head. Now I know that among the twelve of us there have been mutterings. James was with us when we saw the unfortunate event at the Temple when Jesus overturned the tables of the money lenders.

James, son of Zebedee, asks how could we challenge the actions of the Master? It was he, after all, who has taught us all we know. Jesus has shown us the way; lit up our lives; opened our eyes and minds. Jesus has expounded the philosophy and we have followed. He is omnipotent and the Son of God. Wherever he goes crowds follow him but now that may be for the wrong reason.

It is generally agreed we urgently need another miracle from Jesus to show our followers that he is the Messiah. I do not know how he does all these things – particularly a miracle that will impress the masses?

Simon – the Nationalist - then says his main concern was that we were losing ground among our followers. Jesus is not preaching to the masses in the way he used to do and there have been no new miracles. What Jesus has to remember is that we now have competitors and without the miracles there is little to draw crowds. Sadly, we got a crowd yesterday – but for all the wrong reasons. Simon says he does not know what got into him.

I agree, I have known Jesus since the very early days and I've never known him display this sort of anger in public. Thomas Didymus – the doubting one – has been very thoughtful while the others spoke and he asks if we thought the devil might have entered Jesus's soul? After all, does he not constantly warn us about that, asked Thomas, if the devil has entered his soul, what can we do? How can we exorcise the devil from the Master who is the one who exorcises the devil from others, asks Thomas? Some suggest Jesus might now be at the end of his ministry and – if he has been corrupted by the devil – might he go on and destroy everything he has achieved in the last two years? Overturning the tables in the Temple was an act of madness which might be demonic.

I brusquely tell Thomas to be quiet but he is not to be silenced and argues that he believes Mary Magdalene might be playing a part in disrupting Jesus. At last we had reached the point that is causing me so much concern. Although I must admit she has been a faithful follower of Jesus since the early days but perhaps she has become more demanding of him.

I slap the table angrily and say: 'Silence Thomas, we have no room for your doubts or fantasies – you have always been against Mary being in our group. You know only too well that Jesus relies heavily on Mary's advice. Even the thought that Jesus might have been corrupted is too much even to consider – particularly by us, his followers, disciples and friends. No! No! No! Chase these thoughts from your mind Thomas or I will believe that the devil has entered *your* soul.' The others mutter in reluctant agreement.

Finally another voice cuts across the group for Judas had quietly entered the room: 'I have a plan,' he says simply. 'It is radical and it has certain dangers – but all of them can be overcome, of that I am sure. Shall I outline these to you?' We all nod in agreement for we will listen to any scheme that might save our ministry.

We listen intently as Judas outlined his radical plan. By the time he has finished, there is a reluctant agreement. Only Thomas speaks out against it and claims it will push Jesus to his very limits.

I am Claudia Procula, Wife of Pontius Pilate the Governor of Judea:

My husband has been angrily pacing the room and I am staying out of the way. It is always the same when we come to Jerusalem and he particularly hates it at Passover. He constantly states he hates the masses and hates the Jews. But above all he hates Caiaphas, High Priest of the Temple and calls him a turd. Pontius knows that Caiaphas will shortly be calling on him to whine in his ear yet again about some slight or other that he thinks Pontius can resolve. I sigh. I know my husband too well and it is like this every time we are in Jerusalem. We both much prefer Caesarea, but for the Prefect it is a duty particularly at Passover – to ensure the Jews pay their taxes and that no one is fomenting insurrection against Rome. He is a good man but sometimes his temper gets the better of him. However, what has never been in doubt is his loyalty to Rome, and some of his actions, which regularly upset the Jews, are carried out with the best interests of Rome at their heart. After all, Caiaphas is responsible for the lives of these poor Jews which, as a Roman, I see as being quite pitiful. Although, let me add quickly, this is not the fault of Rome.

Oh dear, I can hear Pontius slapping the table and shouting, not for the first time that the Jews are their own worst enemies. I fear he has drunk too much wine. Wherever Rome goes across the world, we encourage those we have defeated to accept the Roman way of life which is, even at its worst, far superior to anything they may already have. Yet as my husband says, he cannot get the Jews to accept this.

Pontius has said time after time that we have to look at what happened when Herod Antipas, the ruler of Galilee, built a new capital city. To quell the unrest he had to behead the rabble rouser John the Baptist. At least that is what Herod told me. Alas, the Jews will not give into Rome. Bother. It's going to be one of those days and my husband is saying, 'Did I or did I not bring them water by building an aqueduct into Jerusalem?' And I admit all he got was whining and whinging from that Caiaphas.

In a stupid moment I once pointed out to him that he had used the Temple funds. I wish I had remained silent for Pontius went into a roaring fit and said in no uncertain terms that it was built to improve the lives of the local peasants and, as far as he was concerned, that's what Temple funds were for. And then of course he went into a fit of anger condemning Caiaphas for living in luxury along with his Temple chums who do little or nothing for their own people far less Rome.

I do worry about Pontius' health when he gets into one of his angry outbursts.

I am Caiaphas, High Priest of the Temple:

I live in a comfortable house constructed within a large courtyard and two miles from the city. My post as High Priest has been handed down through my family, a practice that I trust will continue for many years to come. As High Priest I wield a great deal of power as the chief religious authority in Jerusalem. My most important responsibilities centre on the Temple where I control the treasury, manage the Temple police, perform religious rituals and, most significantly, preside over the Sanhedrin which serves as the local Jewish council and court. Of course, I am only too well aware that my powers, some of which are arguably ad hoc, rely entirely on the patronage of Rome and have done since 63BC when Rome's General Pompey captured Jerusalem – thus ending the independent Jewish state of Palestine. By appointing High Priests to serve in the Temple, Rome maintains the religious interest of the Jews and the political interests of its Empire.

And it is here, under the comparative coolness of the trees, that I have called together my most senior and trusted colleagues. The servants have laid out wine and fresh fruit and, as my colleagues gather I have already consumed a long draft which, with hindsight I should probably not have taken. No sooner have my guests sat down than I launch into a tirade. 'The incident at the Temple was too much,' I roar. 'This man Jesus and his followers must be stopped and stopped now, he is a rabble-rouser who seeks to destabilise the population. Why? To what end? Does he see himself as the religious leader of the Jews?' I sit back; the wine is beginning to affect my head.

Then up speaks Silas, the short, stout, overweight man with the eyes of a pig - but I rely upon him totally, as head of the Temple police. He chooses his words carefully. He says that by and large Jesus has not been a great threat and this is the first occasion he has caused us any direct problems. Mostly he promises a life after death which is in a land of milk and honey and this gives the poor some sort of hope. I drink copiously from my silver goblet again.

I remind Silas and the others that this preacher upset the money changers and sellers of birds and that cost the Temple money. What's more, I add, he likened it to a den of thieves and called it "his Father's House". If that is not a direct threat to me – to us – as the Sanhedrin, then I do not know what is.

My head is spinning as I shout again that Jesus must be stopped. The rest of the group look at each other quietly. They have never seen me so angry or quite so drunk but they know I am right. The incident at the Temple was surely a direct threat to overthrow us and take over the very lucrative businesses we conducted.

There are the usual useless muttering and I remind them that we should never forget the appointment of the High Priest is in the gift of Rome – on the recommendation of the Prefect. Good or bad it has turned out to be very beneficial to us and, indeed, the people could not have asked for a better, more benevolent Sanhedrin than they have in me… us… we only have to point out the aqueduct we brought into the city. There is silence in the courtyard and I stupidly drink more wine. Now I am feeling sick but I am also in an expansive mood. Pilate hates me nearly as much as I hate him, I find myself saying, 'Outwardly we appear to get along with mutual understanding and friendship. In fact, we can hardly tolerate being in the same city far less the same room together.' If he thought for a moment that this Nazarene preacher could keep the ordinary people in better order than we do, I have little doubt that Pilate would not think twice before moving to have him installed as High Priest. At least that is my worry and it is something we must stop.

After a time Silas of the Temple police speaks again. 'The followers of Jesus, while they are entirely dedicated to his cause and, let's face it, they do some good in keeping the Jewish community settled, do not always speak with one voice. But you as always are right, there is a threat to the Temple if Jesus calls it "his Father's House". I believe he can be tried for that.'

A breeze gently rustles the trees around the courtyard and I feel a little better. Then I say to Silas, we must arrest him and subject him to a trial with the scribes and the elders present and, as my mind clears slightly, I add, 'How can that be done without arousing possible discontent among the masses, and while he is not in the company of those thuggish fishermen from Galilee?' But trustworthy and loyal Silas speaks up again, 'I believe it is possible to quietly capture him alone – or at best with that woman Mary in the Garden of Gethsemane, immediately after they have celebrated the feast of the Passover, when he will be hot and tired. I can arrange that. I have contacts – but I will need temple silver to ensure this passes without incident. Shall we say 30 pieces of silver?' There is excitement in my slurred voice and I tell him he can have double that if he must. But I counsel him to make sure he brings this Jesus of Nazareth to a point where he will no longer pose a threat to my rule – our responsibility is what I mean – to the Temple. The others agree and quickly leave.

I pour myself more wine and drink it quickly. My position as High Priest is safe and that is all that matters. But wait! I have a thought – might we tell Pilate that in claiming the Temple as 'his Father's House" he is challenging Rome? A feeling of pleasure descends as I reflect on the evening's discussion.

I am Peter, Brother of Andrew:

I am pacing the small room as I am having second thoughts about Judas Iscariot's plan. There are too many chances that it might go wrong. Yet, why should it? The Sanhedrin could not condemn Jesus to death – it is, after all, simply a Jewish council with limited powers. Jesus' outburst in the Temple is something for which they have the power to punish him and, quite frankly, perhaps Jesus deserves it. This overturning of the tables was out of character – but what powers the Sanhedrin have to punish Jesus are limited. Why am I worrying, I ask myself? After all, it was a minor event and would not in any way mean Jesus has to appear before the Prefect of Judea who does have the power of life and death. Anyway, it is no secret that Pilate dislikes Caiaphas, and is probably highly amused at what Jesus did. Yet, I cannot erase this feeling of unease from my mind.

I am Nicodemus, I own the Room where the Disciples meet:

I do not usually eavesdrop on other people's conversations, but I cannot help overhearing the ones they call Peter and Judas . . . Judas is speaking, 'You look worried brother. Nothing will go wrong; I have it arranged – and what's more, I have 30 pieces of silver for my troubles which will help us greatly.' Peter pauses for a moment before asking, 'Are we both working with the same end in mind, Judas? I sometimes worry that you are not, how can I put it, as dedicated – no that's not the word – as sold on God's Word as those of us who joined Jesus from our work as fishermen on the sea of Galilee.'

Although I do not admit it publicly, I am interested in what other groups are preaching and I know Judas is more of a modern thinker than just a follower and supporter of Jesus. He has also admitted he would welcome a revolution against Rome and that is dangerous if heard by the wrong person. I have been told Peter admires Judas for the way he has encouraged Jesus to look at spreading the message to an even wider audience. But I hear Peter telling Judas this time he has gone too far. I wonder what that means?

I am Judas Iscariot and it is my Plan:

It is true I exercise more influence over Jesus than some of the original followers would like. But, to be fair, they are rough fishermen living in poverty and easily swayed by Jesus' simple messages and promises of life after death in a land which, seems to them, to flow with milk and honey. But I pride myself on being a thinker and I have reached the conclusion – and I know others share my view - that Jesus' time as our unquestioned leader has begun to run out. Might I replace him?

Yes, let's keep Jesus as the Messiah, the Son of God, but let's rein him in. Keep him for special occasions as the man to preach to the masses. But when it comes to leading the disciples the time has come for change. In addition, and as a matter of much more importance, I am in love with Mary as is Jesus and, unknown to the others there is friction bubbling between us, not helped by the fact that Mary seems unwilling to choose. Any such conflict will fracture the bond of the disciples and she knows this increasingly worries Jesus. His health has been under a lot of strain with constant travelling and preaching. Mary says Jesus needs a rest as we all do, and she wants time to reflect on who she really loves.

My plan is simple – I need Jesus to be removed from the group for a period of time to allow Mary an opportunity to be alone with me. A spell held prisoner by the Sanhedrin will leave the coast clear. That is my hope.

I carefully consider Peter's outburst, but we agreed we must move on, Jesus has been – and is – our greatest asset, of that there is no doubt. But he is weary and, as the event in the Temple showed, he is becoming unpredictable. He will answer for this before the Sanhedrin. There is little they can do – but the fact that they will be able to call him before them will ensure they have their dignity restored. And when our many followers, not to mention those who we need to join us from those who come to Jerusalem for the Passover, hear of the Sanhedrin's action, they will be outraged and our following will be strengthened. I reassure myself that is what will happen because I have already agreed my plan with Silas of the Temple guard. He has given me 30 pieces of silver for my trouble.

In addition, the Sanhedrin will realise that the undercurrent of resentment following their arrest of Jesus, will mean that the Temple officials will not be able to take any severe action against him. All of which will strengthen our case in front of our followers. However, Peter has become cautious. He is nearly as doubting as Thomas! 'Can you be sure Jesus will come to no harm?' he asks me again. I take a deep breath. 'Harm in the true sense, no. Harm from the indignity of being arrested by the Sanhedrin and taken before them, yes. What I'm saying is, any harm will not be overly physical. And,' I add quickly, 'the advantage to us is that when a Jerusalem crowded with Jews, many of whom are already our followers, realises what has happened then our status in their eyes will rise immediately. There may even be mutterings of an uprising to free him.'

Peter has become excited. 'You'd like that Judas wouldn't you? I don't know why you cannot accept we come in peace. We ask people to believe in a benevolent God who has sent his son Jesus to earth, borne of a virgin, to ask us to live a pure and good life with the promise that one day we will enter the Kingdom of Heaven to enjoy the fruits of eternal life free from strife and persecution.'

But I am aware that if the masses did rise up the Roman soldiers Pilate has at his command would quickly put it down and the carnage would be appalling. The suppression would increase ten-fold. And at that point we'd bring out Jesus to quell the mob with one of his powerful sermons which in turn would pacify Pilate, who, after all, has a certain sympathy with Jesus and our movement. 'Trust me, Peter, I have many contacts in many places in Jerusalem, I know what I'm talking about. I listen and, quietly, I collect the gossip. I will not let you, or Jesus, down. Trust me brother.'

I am Mary Magdalene, a Follower and Friend of Jesus:

It is a warm night and the Feast of the Passover has gone well for Jesus and the 12 disciples, their friends and families. From the 30 pieces of silver Judas has acquired from somewhere, the disciples have been able to embellish their feast. The conversation has been deep and philosophical and Jesus has been at his best. However, as the night has worn on, he has begun to flag and the room has become hot and sticky. Judas moves to where I am sitting and whispers in my ear; he thinks the Master is exerting himself too much. 'See the flecks at the comers of his mouth,' whispers Judas? 'That is a sign I have seen before and it suggests to me that exhaustion is setting in.'

Judas suggests to me to take Jesus for a quiet walk in the Garden of Gethsemane to allow him to regain his calm and rest his mind and soul?' I am only too eager to take up Judas' suggestion. I too am conscious of just how much effort Jesus has put into the evening and I lean over and whisper in his ear. A few minutes later he and I rise from the table and head out into the night.

To my horror a small party of the Temple police turn up. They overpower Jesus and say he will be taken to the home of Caiaphas. The disciples who have followed run away, but I assume they have gone back to the upper room, so I hurry back and look for them – and there they are. 'You know what those Temple Police are like,' I shout breathlessly, 'what can we do?' One by one the disciples turn and silently stare at Judas Iscariot. 'Well, Judas?' Peter says quietly but with anger suppressed in his tone, 'you promised me.' Judas rises from the table. 'I have it in hand, brothers. Trust me,' he says.

I am Silas of the Temple Guard:

I am beside myself with excitement. The preacher from Galilee, the one Caiaphas perceives to be a threat to his control of the Temple, is about to stand in front of him. Caiaphas succeeded his father-in-law Annas as High Priest and he fully intends to pass the honour onto one of his sons, as he has said many times, and no upstart preacher is going to stand in his way. The gate to the courtyard of Caiaphas' house has suddenly opened and my Temple guards roughly push in the bearded Jew they have just arrested in the Garden of Gethsemane. 'Here is your man,' I say. 'No resistance – he came without argument.'

Caiaphas is rubbing his hands together. 'At last I am face to face with the King of the Jews!' Jesus says nothing and silently looks around the courtyard as others – including Annas – appeared from under the shadows of the trees. 'Gentlemen,' said Caiaphas, a note of glee in his voice, 'let me introduce you to the self-appointed King of the Jews.'

As I expected Annas is the first to speak as is his right as the eldest member of the Sanhedrin. 'So this is the man who upset the tables in our Temple and claimed it as his Father's House. I spit on you,' he says loudly. 'The Temple is God's House and we venerate it in the name of the Jewish people. Who are you – a carpenter's son from Nazareth – to upset our established order, particularly in Passover week?' Annas, a vindictive little swine, rises from his seat and strikes Jesus a blow across his face. 'King of the Jews and Son of God indeed,' he shouts, 'you are a fool and a liar. You may convince the masses you are their appointed leader – but you cannot fool the Sanhedrin. We are the leaders of the Jewish faith, the upholders of the Law, and you would do well to remember that.' And again he strikes Jesus.

Servants appear from the house of Caiaphas with flagons of wine and beakers and the priests and the scribes begin to drink and mock Jesus. They abuse him mentally and physically until they tire of their sport and one by one leave.

However, throughout Jesus has remained silent, refusing to answer questions or rise to their taunts. At last Caiaphas orders the Temple guard to lock Jesus up for the night. His interrogation will start again in the morning. But there is something about this man that impresses me.

I am Tiberius Panthera, a Roman Centurion:

Pilate is beside himself with rage. 'What has that blundering fool done?' he roars at me. 'Arrested Jesus! On what authority has he done that?' I am uneasy. I have fought in many wars in many lands for Rome and now that I have grown old I have been sent to lead a guard for Pilate. There has been a black mark against me since my very early days when I proclaimed myself in love with a young Jewish girl while suppressing a revolt at Beit Sahour, near Bethlehem. However, it was pointed out to me in no uncertain way that Romans did not marry local women even if they were with child and in future I should confine my activities to the brothels – which was, after all, what they were for.

I learned my lesson and now I am loyal, not just to Rome but also to Pilate, for we are both men of the world and despite the difference in rank, there is an understanding between us which is almost a bond of friendship. 'It follows the incident in the Temple, when the preacher Jesus overturned the tables of the money changers and sellers of doves,' Pilate says.

'With respect, Excellency, that is within the jurisdiction of the Sanhedrin as it was an incident in the Temple and not an offence against Rome.' Pilate is up and pacing the floor. 'Yes, yes, I know that. But the man Caiaphas is a fool. Does he not realise that if he sentences Jesus, who is seen by that rabble out there as some sort of Messiah, we could have a revolution on our hands? Before the cock crows I want Jesus and Caiaphas brought here. Use the minimum of men and do it just before dawn is breaking so that the rabble cannot see what is happening. The last thing

I need is a revolt – particularly during Passover.' I salute and leave, clear in my mind what has to be done.

Caiaphas is not expecting the rude awakening as I arrive with a handful of Roman soldiers, and burst into his courtyard just as the cock is about to crow. 'I am ordered to take you and the Jewish preacher Jesus of Nazareth to see the Prefect of Judea, Pontius Pilate,' I say. 'You may find it best if you both come quietly before the city wakes.' And with that we set off in silence.

I am Pontius Pilate, Governor of Judea:

That bloody fool Caiaphas is creating problems and I have to sort it. The man is an idiot. I am already up and dressed and have not slept well. I am in a bad temper. 'Caiaphas!' I shout, 'You are a fool, an idiot and a cretin. Have you no brain in that stupid head? Are you trying to start a revolution in Jerusalem by arresting this . . . this preacher? He promises the masses a life after death in some faraway kingdom. The poor love that. All they have to do is live blameless lives and they will be taken to a promised land. It gives them something to think about and it keeps them from believing they are being persecuted by Rome.' I pause for breath. 'Now you have arrested their Messiah. What is going on in that head of yours?' Caiaphas has not expected such a bad tempered outburst from me. But he is a slippery little rat and he will want to win the argument. Slowly and deliberately he begins to speak. 'Excellency, I beseech you to listen carefully to what I have to say. For far from keeping the rabble in order, he is – I believe – about to rise in insurrection against you and, indeed, the Roman Empire.'

'Don't be ridiculous, Caiaphas,' I roar. 'He is a simple preacher, one among many, with a small band of followers he calls his disciples, and they are mostly rough, uneducated peasants plucked from the rabble and several even rougher fishermen from

Galilee. How could they threaten Rome?' Caiaphas is troubled, I can see that and he chooses his words with care. 'He claims to be King of the Jews and his Kingdom of Heaven is where his God sits.' I roar again. 'I know all this you fool. That does not make him a threat to Rome. Like all these other preachers, he peddles rubbish, the rabble lap it up and that suits us does it not?'

A smile begins to cross the little turd's lips, 'But he claims to be the son of a God. He claims immortality and that on his death he will rise to heaven and sit on the right hand of his God. That makes him a threat to both of us. Remember, that when he overturned the tables in the Temple, he called it his Father's House. Does this mean he wants the rabble to treat him as the High Priest?'

At last I have it – he is worrying for his own position at the Temple and then trying to present it to me as a threat to Rome. I tell him in no uncertain terms he must handle this himself. 'By arresting Jesus, you fool, you have already caused a situation that may erupt at any moment. I strongly urge you to set him free now and perhaps give him some of your Temple silver for the distress you have caused. But the little turd shakes his head. 'You do not understand Excellency. If he is the son of a God and if the rabble believe him – and I think they do – they will follow him. Before long, the whole of Judea could be plunged into conflict. How many soldiers do you have? Can you keep order in Jerusalem and send troops to Galilee?'

Now I am thinking quickly. Could an army be despatched with orders from Rome? Caiaphas allows a smile to briefly cross his lips as he realises what I am thinking – might he be right?. This is his final throw of the dice. 'Governor, you must execute Jesus now as an example to the rabble here in Jerusalem for Passover. They need to know that claiming to be the son of God is a threat to the established order and that Jesus and his gang are simply trying to gain power in Judea,' he says firmly. 'What,'

I exclaim, 'execute Jesus? You are mad Caiaphas. I would have a riot on my hands before sunset if I even contemplated that.'

Caiaphas nodded. 'But Excellency, he is a threat to Rome. You must ask him yourself if he is truly the King of the Jews and if he says yes, then he surely is a threat not just to you but also to Lucius Pomponius Flaccus, the Imperial Legate of Roman Syria. Soon the whole of the region could be in turmoil.' And then he added slowly: 'But if you would rather I took the matter out of your hands and passed it to Flaccus, it could certainly remove the burden from your shoulders.'

I have always known Caiaphas to be a devious swine but I had to admit on this occasion he had me cornered. If the matter goes to a higher authority it will undermine my position here in Judea and might even lead to my being recalled to Rome. And that thought does not please me. This is a comfortable outpost and I enjoy a few bribes from Caiaphas with Temple silver when he needs me to look the other way – but I cannot do it in this case. Then there is the palace by the sea in Caesarea. No, the matter must not get to the attention of Flaccus. If Jesus has to be crucified, it has to be done as quickly and as quietly as possible. If he is immortal – and I doubt such claims – then he will surely reappear among the rabble. If, on the other hand, he is mortal, then other steps would have to be taken.

I turn the matter over in my mind before sending for Tiberius Panthera. 'I need to crucify the preacher Jesus Christ,' I explain simply when the centurion and I are alone. 'How quickly can it be done? It needs to be done right away, and we need to ensure the body is down before dawn tomorrow.' He says there is a cross ready at Golgotha for the robbing swine Barabbas. 'We could send Jesus to Golgotha in place of Barabbas. It would attract little or no attention and we could deal with Barabbas later.' A sense of relief descends upon me. 'Excellent,' I reply quickly. 'I knew I could trust you.'

I am Tiberius Panthera a Centurion. I will arrest the Preacher:

I have my contacts in Jerusalem who keep me informed. There is a man, a devout follower of Jesus' ideas and philosophy who is discontented. He wants the movement to change. I believe he thinks Jesus is preaching and converting the wrong people. He feels that the movement should be trying to convert Rome to their beliefs. His name is Judas Iscariot. Pilate laughs loudly when I tell him. 'Convert Rome to follow the beliefs of a preacher from Nazareth who believes in only one God. What madness! However, if this fits our purpose Tiberius, bring him to me. If you think for a moment Iscariot cannot be trusted, then you know how to use your sword.' I bow and leave.

I am Claudia Procula, Wife of Pilate:

'You are not going to crucify Jesus,' I cry to my husband. I have never ventured to say this to my husband before, but now I tell him, 'This is wrong, very wrong. Jesus does good things and he heals the sick with his miracles. I was so hoping that we might ask him, once Passover is behind us and he is still in Jerusalem, to heal the crippled foot of our dear son Pilo. Please Pontius, please save him even if it is just for the sake of little Pilo.'

My husband is in a foul mood and snaps back, 'He is just an ordinary man and he cannot heal the sick far less create miracles. It is all an illusion and these poor fools out there, who are desperate to believe anything that makes their wretched lives better, believe him. His man Iscariot works the crowds and explains the unexplainable – the rabble believe him.'

'But did he not raise Lazarus from the dead?' 'No,' shouts my husband, 'Lazarus was simply dead drunk – and given time and clean water would rise again. Then Jesus allegedly walked on water on the Sea of Galilee but the bow of the boat was stuck on a small sand bank. These are not miracles!' And I know that my husband truly believes that if they were to become Romans rather than Jews they would enjoy a much better way of life. But they are stubborn as well as stupid and while they remain that way, they will follow their own preacher before accepting what will one day be inevitable and that is to follow the ways of Rome. I look at my husband for a moment. 'But what about the story he fed five thousand people with five loaves and two fishes?'

Pilate is beginning to become exasperated by my questioning. 'That has been explained by Lucius Annaeus Seneca the elder', my husband says quietly as if talking to a child, 'but you probably would not understand it. Jesus was preaching to the mob about the movement of the equinoxes with Pisces being represented by a fish whereas Virgo represents wheat. He was feeding them science, not food! It is what is called a parable and that scoundrel Iscariot has been spinning stories to the rabble about that and they have interpreted it as meaning he fed 5,000 with loaves and fishes. Complete nonsense, of course, but believed by the simple-minded.' 'Oh,' I say a vague look crossing my face. My husband was right, I do not understand it!

I am Judas Iscariot and my Plan is working:

It is not that I would normally trust Pilate who has a reputation for being devious and harsh; I have little choice. He also states that Jesus is a mortal like the rest of us. Clearly someone – probably Caiaphas – has backed the Governor into a corner. The plan I discussed with Silas seemed to make sense for everyone – and Silas said Pilate had agreed to it. But just to be sure, I have had a second plan in mind. Armed with two large flagons of wine and some Temple silver I make my way to Golgotha to see the two sentries who have been left guarding the body of Jesus on the cross.

A crucifixion is never a pretty site. But I am moved to tears as I look up at Jesus my friend, bruised and bleeding from his rough handling by the Sanhedrin and the soldiers. Dried blood masks one side of his face and other abrasions cover his body and legs. I fall to my knees and cry, 'Oh Jesus, forgive me.' But the figure on the cross is only semi-conscious and makes no reply. However, I note with satisfaction that Pilate has carried out his side of the bargain. Jesus is bound to the cross by hemp, the destructive nails that cause agony to so many crucified by the Romans, have been neatly driven between Jesus' fingers and through the hemp at his ankles and have not entered his body. Nor have his legs been broken, all of which means that Jesus has been spared the pain of a normal crucifixion and can also be removed from the cross quickly.

Swiftly I go about my business giving first one and then the other guard a flagon of wine and one piece of Temple silver. The guards are clearly confused, they have been given no orders about this – but they realise I am not hostile, offering only wine and silver and asking for nothing in return. Well, I ask myself, how could a poor Roman soldier say 'no'? Soon I am on my way back across Jerusalem to meet the other disciples. There is much agitation within the group and I immediately feel an air of hostility as I walk into the room. 'Well?', queried Peter immediately. I reply, 'All is going to plan, soon we must make for Golgotha and cut Jesus down.' I smile briefly. 'I do not think the guards will cause us much of a problem.'

As usual Thomas is being negative. He points out that if we bring Jesus back here we are bound to be discovered and then we shall all end up on the cross. I sigh loudly. 'Thomas, Thomas you doubt too much. I have already arranged for him to be taken to an empty tomb belonging to Joseph of Arimathea.' The others are startled at this revelation. 'Joseph of Arimathea is a rich man; surely he is very closely associated with the Sanhedrin', Thomas says. 'Is this a wise decision, Judas?'

Rather testily I point out to Thomas it is true Joseph of Arimathea is a rich man – but I know for a fact he is disappointed by the actions of the Sanhedrin in running the Temple. I also know that he is very taken by the preaching of Jesus and that he supports our cause. Indeed, it may be that he will soon become one of our new and powerful supports. Thomas is not convinced and shakes his head. 'I just hope you are right, Judas. I just hope you are right.'

The night is hot, sticky even, when I set off again for Golgotha accompanied by Nicodemus and the dutiful Mary who carries ointments as well as cloth to bind Jesus wounds. 'Look,' I say, 'Jesus looks a lot worse than he really is. The Sanhedrin treated him very badly – but I do not think he has any broken limbs and his wounds tend to be fairly superficial.' I urge Mary, to go to the tomb and wait for us rather than see Jesus on the cross. As we approach the site I congratulate myself on the planning. The guards are soundly asleep, the wine flagons empty. 'Quickly,' I say to Nicodemus, 'cut him down. He is bound with hemp and the nails have been placed in such a way as not to penetrate his body. Then we take him to Joseph's tomb where Mary will tend his wounds. Then we will roll back the stone to stop intruders.' I have arranged for one of the disciples' wives and a trusted follower to prepare and take food each night to the tomb. In a few days Jesus will be strong enough to travel.' I am aware of an unease among the group and Peter asks, 'But what will we tell the people? They will expect to see Jesus. And the Romans – they will ask also.' I worry sometimes about the stupidity of some of the disciples!

I am Jesus Christ the Son of God:

I have been scourged, tortured and vilified and now finally I am crucified. Shortly my soul will ascend to heaven where I will sit on the right hand of my Father. I will not die as other men die and my body will assume the form of an ordinary man. I forgive Judas Iscariot for he knows not what he has done.

The time has come for Jesus the Son of God to cease to be the Messiah in Judea and for others to spread the Word of God across the earth. I have given the message my Father gave to me; now others must carry it to all mankind.

I am Judas Iscariot, now a humble and penitent Disciple:

Jesus was not supposed to suffer the way he has. While it is dark Nicodemus and I take him down from the cross and remove him to the tomb of Joseph of Arimathea where Mary will tend his wounds while he recovers.

But my dream has crumbled. I can see that Mary's concern for Jesus is that of devotion, so she has made her decision. Also, my hope of becoming the leader of our group has also faded; clearly the other disciples will not trust me again. I must become a penitent for letting my urge for greed and power overtake me

The absence of Jesus will be noted, and we will tell the multitude that Jesus has been resurrected and gone to sit on the right hand of his Father in Heaven. To the Romans we must simply say that Jesus died on the cross and his body is safely in a tomb. So I have told them, 'You must deny all knowledge of Jesus except that he has gone to his Father in Heaven and may return again one day.' For the rest of you, carry on with the mission. I believe it must be to the four corners of the Empire. We must grow our group and deliver the message that there is only one

God – and to achieve a place in the Kingdom of Heaven means leading the life that Jesus preached.

'I have a question,' says Mary, 'where shall Jesus and I go when we leave here, Judas? We have no money and we are simple people with few skills.'

I throw a small leather pouch on the table. 'Mary, the Sanhedrin gave me Temple silver and there remains in this bag 25 pieces. You and Jesus must take it and go to Gaul where friends of the fishermen will help you.' I smile as tears run down Mary's cheeks. 'And Mary,' I add, 'have many children!'

THE BATTLE O' THE BUNNET

'Keep yer hat on,' said the auld wife, *sotto voce*, like.

'It's no' a hat, it's a bunnet.'

'It's a hat: keep it on.'

'Naw.'

'Dae as I tell ye,' her voice now more *voce* than *sotto*.

'For why?'

'I've a good mind to skelp yer lug.'

'Listen hen, if you skelp ma lug I'll skelp yours back twice as hard.'

'Folk dinnae want tae see yer scabby heid while they're at their tea.'

'It's no that scabby; its mair scratched.'

'It's scabby. Keep yer hat ON.'

'Naw. I need it to dicht ma tea. Ony road – it's a bunnet.'

'You'll no' be dichting ony tea in here, my man, in the Co-operative Tea Rooms. Have ye no manners?' Others turned and looked.

Her husband deliberately and carefully decanted tea from the Co-operative Association's china cup into his saucer, wafted his hat over it and delicately raised it to his lips.

'*Slurp*. That's better. I've had a drouth on me aw through the service.' And with that he replaced his bunnet.

'Yer a heathen,' declared his wife, a note of disgust in her voice. 'I dinnae ken why I married you.'

'Aye ye do,' smiled her husband. 'Ye were up the duff.'

'By you, ye dirty bugger. Ma faither was goin' tae kill ye if we didnae get married quick.'

'Aye, only after he'd killed you.'

A banging from the top table cut through their conversation.

'For Airchie McGuire,' said the minister, 'a moment for personal reflection.'

'Get yer hat aff,' whispered the auld wife.

'You've just telt me tae pit it on. An its a BUNNET.'

'Will ye dae as yer telt? It's a mark of respect for Airchie.'

'Did we no dae respect in the kirk?'

'Aye, this is mair respect,' said the auld wife grabbing at her husband's hat.

A short silence fell across the room followed quickly by waitresses placing plates of sandwiches on the tables. 'There's scrambled egg and cress, salmon – it's tinned I'm afraid – cucumber and some with meat paste. Sorry aboot that but we're still experiencing war-time austerity,' said the waitress, 'Mair tea?'

As the husband stretched out to help himself, the auld wife smacked his hand. 'Manners,' she said, picking up tongs to serve him. 'One of each and dinnae eat them as if you'd never seen food before.'

'They're afa' small,' said her husband as he peeled back the bread from the neat triangle containing meat paste. 'This looks like shite,' he said putting the bread back together and pushing it to the edge of his plate before picking up the cucumber. 'Whit did the lassie say this was?'

'Cucumber.'

'It looks like shite and aw.' And again it was pushed to the side of the plate.

'Watch your tongue,' snapped the auld wife, 'here's the minister coming.'

'He's got a face like a smacked arse,' observed her husband.

'It's high blood pressure,' whispered his wife.

'Aye frae chasin' aw the young mothers. I ken, I've heard the stories.'

The auld wife kicked her husband hard under the table.

'Aw Minister that was a lovely service. Airchie would have enjoyed it.'

'Thank you,' smiled the minister piously, 'but Airchie is in a better place and enjoying the love of our Saviour and drinking the wine of contentment.'

'Bless you Minister,' said the wife. 'Ye aye ken whit tae say.'

'Are you enjoying your tea?'

'Oh aye, the Co-op Tearooms aye dae a good purvey,' replied the wife quickly and glared at her husband daring him to utter a word.

'Airchie will be really happy, then,' said the husband smiling. 'If there's wine that is. Airchie aye enjoyed a drink. Preferred whisky to wine mind . . .' But his observations were interrupted as his wife's foot again connected with his shin.

'I dinnae ken whit yer daein wi yer fit,' said the husband, 'but that's ma artificial leg. The other half is still at Anzio.' And he laughed loudly.

Whether the sandwiches tasted like shite or looked like it had suddenly become of no consequence to the husband who had proceeded to clear the plate even eyeing up an adjoining table where the occupants had failed to make inroads into their sandwiches.

'Don't you dare,' said the wife observing his eyes and reading his mind.

'They'll go tae waste.'

'No they'll no, the staff will eat them.'

'The staff didnae ken Airchie. This is for his pals.'

The husband sat back in his chair and burped loudly.

'Yer a pig,' observed the wife.

'Aye I probably am,' replied the husband contentedly.

'If ye were a child I'd tan yer backside.'

'Oh goody,' said the husband, 'it's a long time since I've had any fun doon there . . .'

'Stop that filth,' cried the wife, suddenly conscious that people were looking round. 'Filth, that's all ye have between your ears. Now we're goin' hame so keep yer hat ON!'

'I cannae pit it on,' replied the husband with a smile on his face.

'Why for no?' asked the wife.

Suddenly the husband burst out laughing as he gently opened up his folded bunnet, 'It's they sandwiches from the other table. I thought I could tak them home for ma tea!'

GOODBYE, MR FOGGET

Our hot air balloon is no more than a small splash of colour on washed-out denim above the Valley of the Kings. It hangs motionless, casting a shadow on the bleached landscape, hovering and hissing rhythmically as gas from the burner heats the air in the crimson and gold envelope. With enormous skill it is being controlled by my companion Phileas Fogg who has agreed to take me on my final journey. The only other movement is the occasional flash as the sun bounces off Philey's tall, cream, silk hat. He is, as you would expect, dressed in a neatly-pressed, blue frock coat, checked trousers and polished boots with white spats. I, Phil Fogget, am in my yellow silk pyjamas.

As I peer down I am aware of movement from the tomb of Tutankhamun and I watch as he emerges from his tiny resting place.

'Quickly Philey,' I shout, 'Go. GO! He has doves. I'm not ready for doves.' Ancient Egypt dissolves below; but we are rising too quickly and I cannot breath. 'Slow down, Philey, I'm choking, choking...' I claw wildly at my mouth.

The gentle sweetness of Sister Mary welcomes me. 'Now then Mr Fogget let me adjust your oxygen mask. You've been restless again, you poor man.' She fiddles and fusses expertly around my face. 'There now, that's better. Have you any pain? I can ask doctor to increase your morphine drip.'

I slowly shake my head. No pain today. I scan the now familiar surroundings, the pale green walls with stucco embellishments picked out in white, the plaster image of Our Saviour jars - I have long since ceased to be a religious person. The nuns, moving lovingly among the patients, tend to the needs of us who are dying. As hospices go, this one would be hard to beat. But there are no miracles here; this is the end.

Sister Mary is saying, 'We'll make you as comfortable as we can till your time comes to enter the Glorious Kingdom. I could be quite envious, Mr Fogget – except that would be sinful. There now Mr Fogget, that's you all sorted.' I open my eyes to green walls, the crucified Christ . . .

The doctor is leaning over me, lifting my eyelids and murmuring to himself. 'Not long, Sister, but perhaps another injection and increase the oxygen slightly.' There are no reassuring smiles and with business-like intent the pair gather at the bottom of my bed.

Philey is helping me over the side of the wicker basket and we are rising again, the hiss turning to a roar. 'Are you ready for the final journey yet?' asks Philey. 'No, not at all,' I reply. 'I'd like to travel on the Himalayan hill railway from Kalka to Shimla. Remember the journeys we used to make on the "toy train"?'

In a moment I am standing on the Kalka platform and nobody seems surprised at my pyjamas. They are odd people the Indians when it comes to dress. Now I am drifting into fantasy and somewhere in my head a picture is emerging. It is set in the 'old days' and Philey and I are standing on this very platform in our fine military uniforms. By golly, are we not dashing fellows – feared by the Pashtun tribes, bloodied against Afghanistan troops at the Khyber Pass and heroes of the Sepoy Revolt? My mind is wandering . . .

In my hand is a first class ticket. Even in my pyjamas I am perspiring and I long for the cool, clean, green of Shimla. But I am also relaxing gradually and my breathing is much improved. There is something special about Indian railway stations – they bustle. Everything is done at a frenetic pace with noise and cheerful shouting. In addition to the sound there is colour; even our little blue saddle tank engine is garlanded.

It seems I have this compartment to myself, unusual on the crowded railways of India. I can feel our little engine straining against the weight of the six coaches – but grudgingly it begins to move, crossing viaducts that might well have been built by the Romans – but were creations of the British Raj. Stations are slipping by as we clamber up to Shimla, nearly 7000 feet on a track precariously scratched through the hills for 96 miles. We clatter noisily over 800 bridges above beautiful valleys, where pear and pomegranates grow, through cedar and pine forests that smell so sweetly.

At some point the young man who is now seated opposite me has joined the train. He looks a pleasant, reliable soul, European, slim and neatly dressed in a pullover, freshly pressed jeans and polished brown brogue shoes – this is how I used to dress as a young man, casual but smart. He is wearing a clerical collar and that is unnerving. He smiles welcomingly.

'Have we met?' I ask. There is a pause and the smile broadens. 'Would you like us to have met?' I'm not quite sure how to answer, but there is something about him that is comforting, even familiar. 'Are you going to Shimla?' I ask casually. 'I'll go wherever you go,' he replies. 'I'm here to help prepare you for the journey.' This jolts me more than the train tackling a tight bend. 'To Shimla?' I ask. 'No. The final journey,' he replies. 'Damn! Have you come to take me?' I suddenly blurt out. 'I'm not ready to go yet. Anyway, I'm meeting Philey at the end of the track.' The young man shakes his head knowingly. 'No,' he says, 'I'm just here to help you understand the process. Unless of course you'd like to . . .'

I take a deep breath, 'No, good grief, no. Even if you are God – the answer is still no.' The young man's smile is trusting, and somehow I feel I have known him all my life. Which is impossible, because he wasn't sitting there when we left Kalka. But he has one of those familiar faces. 'I'm not God,' he assures me.

Children are waving excitedly as we pull into another old world railway station – and I wave back. I suggest to the young man that we might alight and watch the engine take on water. In all this activity a sense of peace is descending upon me. The young man turns to me and asks, 'Are you without sin?' I am taken aback.

The steam quickly envelopes us as the engineer tests the pressure. I can feel Philey's hand on my arm and he is pulling me into the basket. Thank you Philey, the last thing I need is a troublesome priest.

Sister Mary is tucking in the bed sheet, adjusting my mask and anxiously looking at Father Philip. Her voice is penetrating and I do not like what I hear.

'Is it the last rites, Father?'

'Well now sister do we know he is a Christian? Is he free from sin? Mind you, I'm not sure it matters, for his soul will soon leave us for the Heavenly Kingdom.'

There is a hesitation in Sister Mary's voice. 'Father, do you ever feel envy as you witness a person going over? My, oh my, but how I wish I could meet Our Father just once so that I could understand the great joy these souls will experience.'

'But Sister,' replies the priest, 'you'd want to come back and tell people! We can't afford to lose you, even into the arms of the Almighty. There is much for you to do here on earth. You must contain your curiosity till Judgement Day.'

They both kneel by the bed, their eyes closed, hands clasped, and the priest begins to drone,

> Pater noster,
> qui es in caelis,
> sanctificetur nomen tuum…

My head is bursting and I want to scream but no sound will come, it is as if Clingfilm has been wrapped around my mouth and I fight to sit up. 'You bloody hypocrite priest, there is no

God.' I struggle to put emphasis on the word 'God.' 'Leave me alone. Heaven is an illusion, created to keep the poor and the persecuted under the thumb.' This is more or less how I explained things to the Bishop before Rome ex-communicated me from the priesthood. So how can I now accept the Penance, the Eucharist and finally the Viaticum? I have to fight.

My struggling has alerted Sister Mary. 'Look father,' she says, 'Mr Fogget is struggling to speak. I think I can read the words "God" and "heaven" on his lips. Oh joy, what a pious man. He wants our prayers father. Bless him.'

> Adventiat regnum tuum.
>
> Fiat voluntas tua,

Philey and I are holding fast above a grey, graceless street in 16th century London. It is a mean day and the women and ragged children have wrapped whatever they have around them. Boys play with dogs and chestnut vendors, their braziers glowing, are doing good business. Pickpockets move silently and swiftly through the crowd. Merchants hang from the upper windows of the soulless tenements. A chill east wind picks up discarded rubbish from the stinking street.

Soon the cause of excitement comes into view. It is a rough-hewn wooden cart drawn by two tired and bony horses. The crowd is shouting and jeering at the three priests kneeling in prayer in the straw in the cart. Women scream and men pelt the clerics with rotting vegetables. A boy raises a stick and hits the side of the cart. The metal rims clatter and rumble across the cobbles as the cart continues unhindered and the stick breaks into pieces.

Philey skilfully edges the balloon ahead of the mob to the scaffold; there are three ropes hanging from the wood. The Queen has decreed that the Church of Rome is no longer recognised; those who disobey will pay the price, disembowelling and quartering. I see my priest among the three – but not Sister Mary, thank goodness.

The roar of the rabble reaches a crescendo as first one priest, then the others, dance on the end of the ropes. The sky has darkened considerably and I am feeling sick, suddenly vomiting over the side of the basket onto the swinging clerics.

"Ach, the poor man," says Sister Mary breaking off from prayer. "It's the morphine that does it. I'll just wipe his chin.' The bloody priest is till droning on,

> Fiat voluntas tua,
> Sicut in caelo et in terra . . .

'Stop,' I am screaming. 'I don't want to be fortified by the last rites.

> Panem nostrum quotodianum da nobis hodie . . .

'Can't you hear me? I don't want your prayers. I am a lost soul – can't you understand?' But it is to no avail.

> Et dimitte nobis debita nostra sicut et nos dimittimus debitoribus nostris . . .

Philey and the balloon are hovering above me and thankfully I scramble aboard. Philey has a concerned look on his face and points to the gas cylinder. I realise it won't give us much more. We bump to the ground and I clamber out into Cambridge's Silver Street. So this is the end of the journey?

The young boys are jumping about in excitement. I am laughing too as we trundle towards the Mathematical Bridge, I am sitting in a small wooden cart like a Guy Fawkes and the boys are vying to push it.

As we trundle towards the River Cam I hear a choir in the King's College chapel and they are singing a Schubert piece . . .

> Ave Maria
> Gratia plena
> Maria, gratia plene
> Maria, gratia plena
> Ave, ave dominus . . .

That priest is still rabbiting away,

In nomine Patris, et Filii, et Spiritus Sancti

With every ounce of breath left in my body I scream, 'I do not want succour for I am a heretic in the eyes of all gods.'

. . . Dominus tecum

Benedicta tu in mulieribus

Et benedictus

Et benedictus fructus ventris

Ventris tuae Jesus.

Ave, Maria.

ASHES TO ASHES

The aging Canadian woodsman views the seasoned ash tree, doubt in his eyes. Why must such a fine tree fall? He knows the answer is Chalara Dieback whose fungus is biting beneath the bark, destroying the growth.

The woodsman too is tall, thin and diseased. He is weighted down with safety gear, his high-glow jacket torn and dirty, the rigger boots scuffed at the toes with folds at the ankles.

The Stihl saw sits silently on the sodden soil. The woodsman spits on his hands, he will defy the law and not wear protective gloves. He lifts the saw, pulls the cord and it screams into life. With the care of a craftsman he presents the spinning blade to the bark. It bites, then leaps and there is a squeal as it finally breaks through the bark. Unlike the woodsman who takes medication, there is no anaesthetic for the tree. It must suffer pain.

Too many enemies are attacking trees; the latest is the emerald ash borer. Not a lot is yet known about it but like dieback it is fatal to trees. Just as his cancer will one day be fatal to him. The woodsman consoles himself that by destroying this majestic ash he will help to save thousands more. Yet it is small consolation. Ironically for a woodsman, he hates felling trees.

A breeze blows through the woodland and the tree is crying, its leaves falling like tears onto the woodsman and his powerful saw. Other trees also drop tears. Heaven too is showing its affinity and a blatter of rain briefly wets the woodsman's face.

The bright blade of the saw is toiling – it is the final moment. The tree screams out as the last sinews snap and she topples, like a hopeless drunk, outwards and downwards to the ground.

As the tree crashes, branches break and jump in the air; a final death throw. In the distance there is a fire where all dead trees are cremated. Chalara Dieback demands this; it is the trees unchallenged fate. The woodsman switches off the Stihl saw and pushes back his hard hat.

Ashes to ashes, dust to dust . . .

THE RITUAL AND THE LADDIE

Slurp! Pause. *Slurp, slurp!* The Auld Yin was drinking his tea from his saucer again. The Laddie pressed his chin down on the old oil-cloth table cover and sighed. He'd seen the ritual many times before, but it never failed to captivate him. *Slurp! Slurp!*

The ritual, of course, required the co-operation of The Wifie; a little old lady who took tiny steps around the kitchenette because she suffered from phlebitis. She didn't shuffle, no; it was little steps she took in her battered tweed baffies, one of which had burn marks on it. The Wifie wore glasses and one eyepiece was a smoky grey, while behind the other lurked an enormous eye, its size exaggerated by the magnification of a thick lens. On the occasions The Laddie spoke, he was conscious of The Wifie's head slowly turning in pursuance of the sound and the great eye descending slowly upon him.

Slurp! Slurp! Soon it would be time to start again. The Auld Yin was a proud man, slightly bent by toil; he was a cooper to trade. He had worked hard all his life and now he was the foreman. He and The Wifie were proud of that and saw it as a reward for all the years of struggle.

Anticipation was growing for The Laddie. The saucer was nearly empty. One more powerful *slurp* would do it. The Wifie fussed around the black range, one foot inside the fender among fallen hot ashes, the other outside on the polished linoleum.

But something had gone wrong and The Auld Yin was rising from the table and clutching his evening newspaper which had been propped between the jar of home-made jam and the edge of his plate. 'I'm tae the closet, wifie,' he said as he walked determinedly to the kitchen door.

The Wifie was clattering around with the big kettle. Pouring hot water into a teapot and swirling it round before pouring it down the sink. Excitement began to mount again for The Laddie as he realised the ritual was about to start from the very beginning. This was going to be worthwhile.

One, two, three tea spoonfuls of tea. Just the right amount. After all, The Auld Yin had been working hard all day, in the cold and dusty brewery next door so several cups of tea would be required to restore his spirits. The kitchen door opened again and The Auld Yin came in clutching his newspaper and looking relieved. 'Aye wife,' he said and nodded; no more words were needed in this tried and tested scene, played out over many years as he took his seat back at the top of the table

The cup was on the saucer, a small jug of milk placed nearby and a spoon stuck out of the filled sugar bowl. 'Right wifie,' said the Auld Yin without lifting his eyes from the newspaper which was again propped safely between the edge of his plate and the top of the jam. 'Aye,' she said by way of reply. They both knew the routine. The Laddie waited eagerly for the sound. *Slurp! Slurp!*

The Wifie shook the teapot round and round a couple of times as if invoking some magic then slowly and with a skill practised over many years, filled the cup. The Auld Yin looked up from his paper and nodded. 'Thanks wifie,' he muttered and the muscles in his cheeks tightened to produce a weak smile. Reaching for the milk jug he splashed a touch of its contents into the cup, followed by a little sugar. The Wifie stepped back while the Auld Yin carefully lifted the cup and poured half the contents into the saucer.

The Laddie felt his bladder twitch and he involuntarily grasped his crutch with his right hand. Excitement and anticipation had this effect on him. Now came the most important aspect of The Ritual. The Auld Yin removed his battered tweed cap, always referred to in the family as The Bunnet, revealing the pure white, thinning hair that sparsely covered his shinning pink scalp.

With the ease of a great artist finally flicking his brush across a masterpiece, The Auld Yin wafted The Bunnet over the saucer. To the right, then slowly back again. He had a look of great intensity on his face, as if his life depended on this act. To the right, then back again; to the right then back again. He stopped and looked hard at the saucer. Satisfied, he placed The Bunnet back on his head and with both hands he carefully lifted the saucer to his lips . . . *slurp! slurp!* Pause. *Slurp! Slurp!*

THE PRAM, THE PIGLET AND
MAGGIE THE MAID

The Hon. Lady Marigold Petunia Lily Budd, the 22-year-old youngest daughter of the noted Victorian plant collector, the Marquis of Barra and Mingulay, is pushing a large and stoutly built perambulator around the grounds of a Lunatic Asylum. The perambulator contrasts unsympathetically with Lady Marigold's slim frame. She has stopped at the beginning of a woodland path to adjust the blankets and mutter, in soothing tones, the words familiar to all mothers. As she leans over the perambulator Lady Marigold's long dark hair falls like a curtain across her pale face. There is no baby in the pram – only a piglet.

Dr Theodore Smillie, the Medical Superintendent, is looking down from his window in the fine biscuit-coloured sandstone building he has had built on the top of the hill. This new building mostly houses paying patients from the upper classes, who look to the eminent psychiatrist for a 'cure.' It is a secluded place, offering discretion, calm surroundings, wholesome food (Dr Smillie is very insistent on this), music, fresh air and sometimes even recovery.

Lady Marigold is accompanied by her maid, Maggie, a big, ruddy cheeked, lassie from the country. It is Maggie's job to attend to the needs of Lady Marigold and, although she is only semi-literate, Maggie religiously writes home to her mother; Maggie may be with child but does not yet know it.

'Good progress being made with Lady Marigold, I think Urquhart,' says Dr Smillie after a few moments of observation. 'What is our next move would you say?'

Urquhart, principal assistant to the eminent psychiatrist, rubs his chin and pauses before answering, 'The plan of placing a piglet in the empty pram so that Lady Marigold might reject it does not appear to be working. Sadly, she treats the piglet like a baby. We've tried removing the covers from the pram, but still allow Lady Marigold to push it round the grounds in the hope she would get fed up; that has not worked either. I still consider the head of a dead pig would sicken her. We need her to reject the pram and its contents.'

'I was reading her case notes again,' says Urquhart. 'Was the child born alive?'

'Yes, the family had it removed immediately after birth and homed with a childless couple on the Marquis' Derbyshire estate, far away from Scotland and Lady Marigold. It will be well looked after and the Marquis has arranged a generous allowance to the new family.'

'Was there no question of marriage?'

'Sadly not. The father was an under-gardener and while he was eager to wed Lady Marigold, the Marquis felt this was not a suitable match. Sad, really, I always feel a child benefits from having both parents around it. The lad was sacked without a reference, so his future looks pretty grim unless he joins the army.'

'And she suffers melancholy and attempts at suicide as a result of this separation from her child and her love?'

'I fear so, Urquhart. But we are making progress here. However, she must be encouraged to eat more. As you know my philosophy is that plenty of nutritious food aids recovery from mental mania.'

'Yes, I've noticed she doesn't eat much. Her maid does! Eats like a horse and I suspect consumes some of Lady Marigold's as well. I've noted that on the file.'

'Keep an eye on the maid, Urquhart, I believe she may be forming a relationship with that cheeky pot boy in the kitchen and I don't want any unnecessary liaisons, or complications, between the two.'

Goodhope House
May 1893

Dear Ma,

I hope this finds ye weel. This is a grand plase we ar in an Lady M is doing wel to.

It's a braw builing mair like a big hoose for the gentry than for loonies. I have my own wee room in anither bit ow the plase. Reel cumfie Ma I can tel ye. Lots o grub an awe. Lady M dusnie eat much so I geed her a wee hand and am getting as fat as a pig.

The doctors hae takin the doll frae the pram noo and Lady M disnae ken. Its awe part of ther plan tae mak her better. She is a bit kamer than when we cam heer. But Ma I get bored as awe we do is wauk roon the groonds wi her pooshin the pram and cooin awa at the bairn that's no there. But I get pade weel so I cana complain muckle.

I miss you Ma an the dug. Has she had her pups yet? I canna mind wen she is dew.

There are sum rite daft bugers her rite enuf. The Majur is aye tryin to get booz and evun askit me tae smugle sum in fur him. I telt him no as Id get kicked oot by the docturs. Ther is a wifie who dresis reel daft an rites potri. They ar awe loonies Ma.

Ive met a reel nice lad hoo wurks heer an he saz he luvs me. Whatz happenin wi yoos? Rite soon.

Aw mi luve,

Maggie XXX

Major the Honourable Guthrie Crumley, MC, is dying for a drink. There is nothing new in that and he is hunting around the grounds in the hope of finding someone secreting alcohol about their person. He has espied the padre sitting in the sunshine considering his sermon before ministering to his flock in the asylum. Major Crumley heads in the direction of the Reverend in the hope this man of God may have a secret stash of church wine. He stops in front of the minister and leans over, 'I say old boy I don't suppose you have any church wine in your room?' Dr McCarry looks up, 'You shall have no other gods before me . . . and that goes for communion wine as well. Exodus chapter 20 verse 3 if you want to look it up.'

High up in the main building Dr Smillie is observing the scene. 'The major is heading towards the gate Urquhart. If he reaches the town drink will be taken.'

'He knows he will be discharged immediately if he is found to have been drinking. I've made that clear to him. His family have confirmed he will then be cut off without a penny.'

'He has stopped.'

'Good.'

'Not good. He is talking to the milk delivery boy no doubt trying to bribe him to bring in alcohol. We need a solution, Urquhart.'

'But what, sir?'

'Just that . . . a solution. One that looks like alcohol, smells like it but makes him terribly sick. Put it in an empty gin bottle . . . But first try some opiates in his orange juice. 'Ah, the milk boy is making a rude gesture. I think the major's plan has failed. Good.'

Goodhope House
September 1893

Dear Ma,

Theye pit a wee piggy in Lady Ms pram the ither day wraped in a shawl and shee fel in luve wi it and caries it aboot we her singin wee songs. Im beginin to think she is a loonie. Onyroads the pig is getting biger and is shitin al over the plais and a dokter cam in the ither day and skitit on his erse. No very pleased I can tel ye.

Ma this lad I met is richt braw and sez he luvs me and wants tae get mairit. His name is Erchie and I like him. He has askit the dokters if he can get the job as the gatekeeper heer and a wee hoose gos wi it to. Imaj in me mairit Ma. Yool like Erchie.

Must go as Erchie is takin me intae Embra for the day. Stil pitin on the beef and nearly as fat as Lady Ms pig.

Rite soon

Aw ma luv,

Maggie xxx

Hilary Beatrice Solomon, a minor member of a major brewing dynasty, likes poetry, and walks around the grounds reciting. She is particularly fond of William Wordsworth and believes he was once her lover. Miss Hilary also writes poetry but not as well as Wordsworth. Most recently she has read work by William McGonagall, a poet and tragedian, whose unusual style has attracted a certain interest among the literati. Miss Hilary has advised her doctors that she intends to find fame by emulating the styles of Wordsworth and McGonagall. The doctors have noted she is greatly enthused by the idea; mania has receded and her appetite returned. The doctors are encouraging her in this work and have supplied her with paper, pens and ink.

Miss Hilary is an eccentric in her dress and style. Her colours for skirts and blouses are bright, often combining strong browns, reds and greens with yellows, blues and pinks. Her hair is clean but unkempt and she wears sandals in all weathers. She has expressed a desire for freedom of mind, spirit and dress and to go where she wishes in the extensive grounds. She has no maid to help her, but a family trust pays for her care.

Today she has encountered Lady Marigold pushing the neatly wrapped piglet in the pram, and Maggie, as they walk through a tunnel of greenery.

'I wandered lonely as a cloud that floats on high o'er Vales and Hills when once I saw. . . no, that's wrong. . . when all at once I saw a crowd. . . that's it you see, I missed the 'all at' bit sorry I talk too fast how is the baby?'

Before she could reply, Maggie said, 'Your pen – its dripping ink onto your dress and that will no come oot.'

'Don't worry young lady I'm a great poet and ink on my dress is so natural oh the baby is very fresh and pick I think I'll write it a poem about him or her what do you think Lady Marigold you don't mind if I call you Marigold do you it's just I don't know your surname and oh what a funny noise your baby is making it sounds like a squeak. . .'

'It is a squeak,' said Maggie. 'It no a bairn. . .' she hesitates and bites her lip.

By now Lady Marigold is pushing the pram further into the woodland, her hair closing around her face, shielding her from the world.

Dr Smillie removes his pipe, 'Urquhart, the Solomon woman; she's button-holed Lady Marigold. Will her ranting about Wordsworth inflame Lady M's mania do you think?'

'Not while she has her maid with her – but it is a cause for concern. By the way, that maid is getting as fat as a pig. . .'

'Or fatter than the piglet, eh, Urquhart? The piglet -- in the pram, what!'

'Indeed, sir. Very droll. We are going to have to do something about that piglet. It's growing up fast and it's leaving excreta all over the damned place and it is beginning to stink quite badly.'

'Yes, I know, Urquhart. Didn't quite work out the way we expected. I still say we should have put a dead pig in the pram. Trouble is, if we move it now the melancholy will return possibly with mania and morbidity. We cannot risk it but we do need an answer. Is that maid girl still fraternising with the kitchen boy? Are we going to give him the gatekeeper's job? He could probably do that. Getting a bit old for the kitchen. He has no education but it's not a cerebral job. Fix it Urquhart.'

Hilary Beatrice Solomon is busy writing. . .

> *You wander lonely with the child*
> *and float on high o'er paths and hills*
> *you seem so fresh and clean and mild*
> *you bloom just like the daffodils.*

Miss Solomon considers this for a moment, sucking the end of her pen and allowing more ink to fall on her skirt. Then she begins again. . .

> *All hail the bonny lady M*
> *you are the most beauteous fair maid I did ever*
> > *hear or see*
> *a woman kind who glistens bright*
> *and because of that all around you do delight.*

Hilary Beatrice Solomon is delighted with her work and wanders, lonely as a cloud, along the path reading aloud and rereading her latest verse.

Maggie is not feeling well; she has terrible stomach cramps and is pleased when Lady M decides to return to the asylum's main building. Perhaps she can get some bicarbonate of soda from the kitchen. As they reach the steps Maggie's waters burst and she crumples to the ground screaming for her mother.

'Good God, Urquhart. The maid, Lady Marigold's girl, has collapsed and is clearly in agony. Quickly summon help.' And with that the eminent psychiatrist rushes from his room. But he is at loss to know what to do as the girl is obviously in labour and about to be delivered of a child. Dr Smillie has no experience in such matters. 'Quickly, Urquhart, do something.'

Goodhope House
November 1894

Dear Ma,

Iv had a bairn a fine wee ladi wi lungs lik a foghorn. I didnae ken I wuz expectin and Erchie wants tae get mayrit rit noo. He has got the job as gateman and the wee hoos for us. O ma imajin me a mither and you as a granny. Is it no braw. I dinae ken whit Erchie was trying to do but I kent it was a braw feelin.

Lady M wants to cum wi us to the wee hoos and look efter oor bairn. I dinae ken if that can be rite but thatz whit she saz she wants tay dae. Ther is nae muckle room in the cottage but Lady M sez she will sleep wi the bairn and ye ken whit she is lik when she gets an idea in her heid.

Writ soon Ma,
Luv frae Maggie Erchie and the bairn. xxxxx

Dr Smillie sits back and lights his pipe. 'Well, Urquhart, some good results.'

'Indeed, sir, although I'm worried about the situation with Lady M and her maid.'

'Indeed,' replies Urquhart, 'it's a role reversal we did not expect with Lady Marigold looking after her maid's child and living in the tiny gate house with them.'

'Yes. Unusual. But the mania and melancholy have passed and she is happy and eating again. From that point of view, Urquhart, a success.'

'Indeed, sir. The Major is also doing well. He seems to have no urge to drink and he has joined the asylum choir. I must say he has a splendid baritone voice and is the life and soul of the whole asylum. I'm just keeping up the level of opiates in his orange juice. He may become addicted to these. . .'

'But at least he's off the drink, Urquhart, and that's what matters. Why, half of China is on opiates and bringing in a pretty penny for British business at that.'

'I've also told Miss Solomon we will publish her anthology if she completes it soon. Happy lady.'

'We've done it, well done, Urquhart. A sherry?'

'Why not, Sir. A toast to success.'

MEDDLING WITH MRS MARTHA MAITLAND'S MIND

Mrs Martha Maitland, formerly of Braidwood House, Kinglassie, Fife, widow of Mortimer Maitland, mine owner, is sitting on the edge of her bed studying nothing, Nothing is a good thing to study for it is nowhere and Mrs Martha Maitland's mind seeks to be nowhere, studying nothing. If she is nowhere studying nothing she understands she is safe from everything, such as people and sounds and smells and problems. Everything! That is why Mrs Martha Maitland remains closeted in this world of nowhere, while studying nothing.

Therefore, because in her mind she trekked across hostile territory, fought wars, been persecuted and her soul invaded by demons, she finally decides she must find sanctuary in her own domain of nothingness and nowhere. Mrs Martha Maitland is unaware that she is surrounded by beauty in the stout sandstone East Lothian building overlooking the sea and surrounded by carefully maintained woodland and freshly cropped grass that has been purpose-built as an asylum with treatment based on the latest thinking by an eminent psychiatrist in nearby Edinburgh. The aim of this place is to provide sanctuary for those who have disturbed minds – and can pay. Happily, Mortimer Maitland (deceased) left Mrs Martha Maitland and the family well-provided for, so that her son and two daughters can sigh with relief that troublesome Ma is well cared for and out of their lives, their consciences cleared.

'Mrs Maitland. Time to see the doctor.'

A bomb has exploded in the land of nothingness. The intrusion is catastrophic and has the same shock effect of stickling plasterer being ripped from an unhealed wound. And immediately the unwanted world is meddling with Mrs Martha Maitland's mind again.

'Now then Mrs Maitland, how are we today?' the superintendent smiles absently, his concentration focused on lighting his pipe, Mrs Martha Maitland looks at the far corner of the large and dingy room. She believes if she concentrates hard she can regain the lost ground that will enable her to recover nothingness and nowhere.

'We have a new treatment, Mrs Maitland,' the medical superintendent says as he shakes the flame from the match he has used to successfully light his pipe. 'It is called electro-convulsive therapy and it is very new. I wonder if you might be willing to try it. My colleagues and I think it will help jolt you back into reality.' But Mrs Martha Maitland doesn't want to be jolted back into reality; she is content with nothingness and nowhere. Her eyes are focussed on the deepest corner of the medical superintendent's room. She closes her mind, cuts out the sound and tramps constantly across the wreckage of life to the safely of nothingness and nowhere.

Mrs Martha Maitland takes a deep breath and closes her eyes, raising her head slowly up and down as she shakes out reality and replaces it with . . . 'That's good Mrs Maitland. Very good indeed. Thank you! I'm sure you won't regret it. A nod indeed was all I needed. Well done! Hoorah for Mrs Maitland! Treatment begins tomorrow.'

Mrs Martha Maitland does not hear him. She has recouped her lost world. She is safe back in nothingness and nowhere.

A death notice appears in the newspapers shortly after:

At peace, Mrs Martha Maitland (1868 – 1925) widow of the late Mortimer, Braidwood House Kinglassie, Fife, much loved mother of Nathanial, Nancy and Norma, after a long illness stoutly borne. Mrs Maitland will be remembered for her sterling work in the community, particularly in relation to her efforts to have advanced medical practices made available to the poor of Fife.

Service of Remembrance at Kinglassie Memorial Church . . .

TWA LADDIES TALKING

Yer sitting on the top o' the dyke.
Aye.
Fur why?
Tae see the view.
Whit view?
That view.
There's nae view there.
Aye there is.
It's just the back o' hooses.
Naw it's naw.
If a could get up there a could see an' aw.
It's fell high.
A ken. But a want tae see whit you can see.
A'll tell ye.
Go on then!
Ye ken big Aggie McCluffy.
Aye. Her that works on the bins?
Aye. Big wuman.
A ken her. Stinks a bit.
Aye and when she comes back she must tak a shower.
Ye ken this?
Naw. But am sittin' here hopin'.
Dinnae tell me ye can see in her lavvie windae.
Aye.
Hae ye seen her yet?
Naw. But am hopin'.
Gie us a hand a want tae see an aw.
BANG. CRASH WALLOP!
Ya silly bugger, Ye've ca'ed me aff the dyke. Now nane o' us 'll
see if Big Aggie is ha'in a shower.
Aye, right enuff.

THE RISE AND FALL OF WILBERFORCE CLUTTERBARN

As the working week withers and before the weekend explodes in colour and noise, there is an interregnum, a hyphen, a plank across the stream – it is called The Pub. And it had become a tradition that we three press officers from the Department for the Preservation of Endangered Trees and Shrubs (DePeTS) shared our reflections on what had just past and what might come, as we washed away the mental grit with the gentle balm of Watney's Red Barrel, a pleasing and popular tipple in 1970s London.

But that Friday we were less animated. Wilberforce Clutterbarn was about to enter our comfortable world. We were apprehensive as none of us knew much about him and what little had seeped out from the Whitehall personnel machine was discouraging. He was, it seemed, a military man, had no experience in the media, a reputation for bluster – and he was due to join us on Monday.

Let me scroll back a bit . . . For more years than anyone could remember, our Director of Information had been a very laid back Londoner, appropriately named Charlie 'Woody' Wood, whose main aim in life was to catch the 5.25 pm from London Bridge (via Greenwich and Westcombe Park) to Erith. Woody was a total convert to long lunches, particularly when paid for by a journalist. Don't get me wrong, Woody was an accomplished spin doctor and like many an old hack that had retreated into the Government Information Service when control of Fleet Street fell to accountants, he could make the most boring project sound exciting. Ours was a happy and successful press office – if one of the backwaters of government.

Then came the day when Woody's timbers began to creak and age to weary him, time swung the axe and full of joy and fine wine, aged 60, Woody was felled from our lives. Then Clutterbarn entered and war broke out.

Our press office was small compared to the great Departments of State and after Woody, the doyen was Jasper Goodfellow, a crumpled, slightly tubby fellow, a veteran of many Fleet Street circulation wars, who claimed to have joined the press office in a bid to save his liver. The truth was he was fired for being in a pub once too often when a story broke. He possessed an over-developed sense of the ridiculous and a vivid imagination – and could sniff a story at one hundred yards. At 11 am each morning he'd cry, 'Jasper's off for a gasper.' When he returned fifteen minutes later there was the hint of tobacco and a strong whiff of alcohol. Thus he became known in our group simply as 'Gasper.'

The fact we all had nicknames had been encouraged by Woody as the sole part of his 'management plan.' He claimed this encouraged 'bonding' so nobody took themselves too seriously. Nancy Pitcairn, a long-time member of the press office, was called Bow-wow. A lady of many summers and numerous affairs was tall, thin and bespectacled whose capacity for sinking whisky, washed down by Red Barrel, was legendary in Whitehall. She was a refugee from the sinking of the Daily Sketch. Then there was me, Harold Tartaglia, known as Tarry Harry. But all this camaraderie was to be destroyed – and more besides - when Wilberforce Clutterbarn walked through the doors of Plan Store House, 66 Whitehall, London SW1.

By some form of telepathy we had arrived early that Monday morning. Bow-wow started it. 'We'd better get this place cleaned up a bit,' she said. 'Look at the piles of paper, directories and, dare I say it Gasper, a half-eaten Indian carry out.' Soon the desks were cleared, an aerosol of polish applied and the waste buckets filled to overflowing. Then Wilberforce Clutterbarn marched in.

'What a bloody mess,' he roared. 'Does nobody clean these offices? You,' he pointed at me, 'I'm appointing you officer-in-charge of getting this office cleaned. Highest standard required. Can't stand an untidy office. I was warned this was a sloppy outfit.' With that he disappeared through the door to his own room.

We had all looked at each other – for a moment dumbfounded. What the hell had all that been about? The first salvo had been fired and we were cowering deep in our trench already. A quick phone call to central services ensured the prompt arrival of two cleaners, one of whom would soon receive a whiff of Clutterbarn's powder as he emerged from his office shouting, 'That bloody woman is smoking. It's a fire risk when handling waste paper. Put it out NOW.' The startled cleaner took a contemptuous puff. 'You wot? I'll get my bloody union onto you. Cheeky bastard. Come on Marj, we're out of here.' And the two laid down their half-filled sacks and headed for the door.

Clutterbarn, his long bony face florid, a vein throbbing on the side of his forehead, cried, 'You, Tartaglia, apprehend these women immediately. They have disobeyed a direct order. Stop them at once.' By the time I made a move the cleaners were well down the corridor leaving only a thin trail of cigarette smoke.

So this was to be our future – led by a deranged soldier, ordered about like squaddies, shouted at . . . oh dear, come back Woody. In fact, we had been so knocked out of our normal routine that Gasper didn't even go off that morning for the first of the day. But worse was to come . . .

Shortly after ten, Marge, the efficient, but easily upset personal secretary to the Director of Information came through and announced that Clutterbarn was calling a company commanders' meeting at 1130 hours. 'You'd better be prompt. An odd stick this one if ever I've seen one. So unlike dear Woody,' and she left suppressing tears.

I had an inclination of what she was talking about. 'It's military speak for heads of units or departments,' I explained.

'Trouble is we don't head anything. Has anyone got shoe polish – I feel a bit of boot-bulling coming on?'

The meeting stripped us as if a plague of locusts had landed on a field of maize, leaving us cloaked only in the skin of our own incompetence. Clutterbarn left us in no doubt his view of our professionalism was nothing short of disastrous. Collectively we were failing in our mission. Our score rate in terms of coverage in the broadsheets was abysmal. Clutterbarn had us tied to stakes and verbally flogged. It was not a good morning. The battle was underway.

However, Bow-wow, a feisty lady, tried to rise to our defence. In a voice full of indignation she declared, 'I have to disagree completely with you Will . . .' But before she could say more he exploded. 'Will! Will! I didn't give you permission to call me Will. It's Mr Clutterbarn or WC - or Colonel. I will not condone this informality and I tell you now – stop using nicknames. It is unprofessional. Now Miss Pitcairn . . .'

But Bow-wow had her gun to the ready and cocked. 'If we are going to be so formal,' she sniffed, 'then I'm MRS Pitcairn, although where that bastard went twenty years ago, I don't know . . . However, the point I was trying to make is – look at the cuttings,' she paused for a moment and then, with all the contempt she could muster, spat out, 'WC - then you would see there is not a week goes by that we don't get good coverage in all the trade and technical magazines.'

Clutterbarn had reached for his pipe and lit a match as Bow-wow attacked. 'That's my bloody point,' he roared. 'What use are trade and technical journals to the Minister. None! They don't bring in votes. The Minster is our first priority. I want to see him on front pages, in weekend supplements, on chat shows . . .' Suddenly WC - I was already picturing the connection between him and a brick-built water closet - realised how close the match was to his fingers and threw it thoughtlessly at his wicker wastepaper basket.

'But,' said Gasper, 'impartiality is how we operate. We work for the ministry. If there is a rare policy decision from the Minister, we make it . . . by the way – I think your basket is on fire!' With alacrity Bow-wow grabbed the water carafe, knocking over the contents of half a glass of water on to WC's papers in the process, and poured the contents roughly into the smoking basket. Meanwhile, Gasper was pulling the red government-issue fire extinguisher from the wall. 'No, no! Not the fire extinguisher,' screamed WC. 'Get out all of you – get out!'

An astute junior civil servant, passing in the corridor and smelling the smoke, hit the fire alarm and the building immediately filled with the crescendo of the claxon, a relic of World War 2. Obedient servants flooded out into Whitehall. But this was at the height of the IRA terrorist threat and soon the street had filled with police vehicles, fire engines and ambulances. A well-regimented company of guardsmen marched quickly from Horseguards and took up position in Downing Street. The cabinet, meeting at number 10 for routine business, retreated swiftly to the basement and an anti-missile weapon appeared miraculously in the Rose Garden. In the Cabinet Office the doors of the emergency briefing room were unlocked as police sealed Whitehall at Trafalgar Square and Westminster Bridge. Even Parliament was locked down and the underground suspended. Worst of all, the Watney's delivery vehicle, destined for the Red Lion, got stuck in traffic even as bored clerical staff were pushing through the doors of their favourite watering hole.

It took two hours for police and security services to satisfy themselves that Clutterbarn's pipe was the sole cause of the chaos and many more for central London to sort itself out. However, we did have one major achievement – our Minister was on the front page of all the news sheets and on radio and television. We even managed to get the Prime Minster involved in the affairs of our department. A first for us. Surely WC would be pleased! First battle won by the home force.

It was several days before WC emerged fully from his office, his time occupied by interviews with internal and external security, the police, MI5 and an assortment of officials from the Home Office. He was, of course, absolved of all blame and the astute junior civil servant who raised the alarm was given an official warning and moved to Registry.

Several weeks passed in which time WC had us write rolling programmes for media announcements, shouted at us on a regular basis and threw files across desks with the remark, 'This needs more work.' But our second victory was not long in coming. WC decided to accompany the Secretary of State to a conference on sphagnum moss harvesting, held in a remote country house somewhere in the North Weald.

This suited our Secretary of State, a Home Counties squire, given his post in our obscure ministry as a thank you for loyal service over many years. He was a big, bluff man of naval bearing. We called him The Walrus because of the nose hairs he never seemed to trim. In fact, he was Sir Bartholomew Blank-Cliff, a hereditary baronet, educated at Eton and the Royal Naval College. The Walrus was not the brightest of politicians – but he had inherited wealth and, with little need of brains, entered Westminster via a safe seat. He and WC got on famously, military men do, but their trip to the North Weald led to a second opportunity to gain unwanted national coverage.

Our account of this event came via the Minister's Principal Private Secretary, Peregrine McClure, who nearly always accompanied the S of S. Gasper's phone had rung about 10.30 am and the breathless Perry spluttered, 'I've lost the minister . . . down a hole.' Gasper grinned, 'But The Walrus is always in a hole.'

'No, no,' said the Perry quickly. 'It's all your bloody boss's fault. He took The Walrus exploring and he fell down a hole.'

'Clutterbarn fell down the hole?'

'No, the bloody Minister. Do try and keep up Gasper.'

'Is he hurt?'

'No – but a trifle dishevelled and a very badly bruised ego. Seems Clutterbarn claimed to know this building, took the Minster down to the basement to show him a tunnel used by Cavaliers to escape Cromwell's Roundheads, not knowing there had been archaeological excavations – and in the half-light poor old Walrus fell down the trench. Trouble was, ground water had begun to seep in and... Well, I thought you had better know in case any of the media get onto it, not that it's very likely as this is hardly a headline event ...'

But Gasper was ahead of him and was reaching for his typewriter. He laid down the telephone, quickly briefed us, and said, 'I feel a story for Peterborough at The Telegraph coming on!' Bow-wow grinned, 'And I'll knock out a piece for Charles Greville at the Mail.' Which only left me to write a paragraph for the Express's William Hickey column.

For some reason, WC was not greatly pleased by the coverage the Minster was getting and his ranting and raving had got worse, not realising we were the media's source. One Friday in the sanctuary of the Red Lion Gasper came up with the final solution that was to see The Walrus retired to the House of Lords and WC to the Crofters' Commission in Inverness.

'I notice The Walrus is to attend a conference in Buenos Aires,' I said by way of conversation. 'I suppose he'll be taking the WC with him – but no other officials, not even Perry – all to keep the costs down.'

Gasper looked long and hard at his glass and Bow-wow said, 'I can see Gasper's mind working overtime. What's with it, Gasper?' A slow smile crossed his face. 'Buenos Aires – Argentina. Do you know that at the end of the war a lot of Nazis escaped to the Argentine on false passports, and set up their own colony? Simon Wiesenthal's Jewish Documentation Centre might just be interested in the Minister's visit. Listen, this is what we'll do ...'

And so it was that The Walrus and the WC were kidnapped by Mossad and taken to a secret location near Buenos Aires. It took the Foreign Office several days to prove their identities and for The Walrus and WC to be released.

Happily, we never saw The Walrus or the WC again.

THE RUSSIANS ARE COMING

There is a fence in people's minds that separates the acceptable from the unacceptable, good from evil, happiness from sadness, white from black, imagination from reality, today from yesterday. Without this fence our souls would wither. We must replenish the spirit with positive thought for this is the fuel that warms the mind.

It is becoming difficult to find the gateway, to stumble through to the positive side, blocking out the unacceptable, maintaining the good, keeping happiness from becoming sadness, white from merging with black, blocking wicked reality from happy imagining, keeping today from intruding violently on yesterday's memories. As the sinews of my body dissolve in a deep pool of pain, day upon day, hour upon hour, keeping to the imaginary side of the fence becomes more difficult; I cry to God in despair. Perhaps He will help and let me drop dead where I stand or not awaken one morning. But not today, I must keep strong, remain on the positive side of the fence. I squeeze every fibre of my fading body to inject more fuel. At last my mind is lit. People are muttering: the Russians are coming.

Is it possible one day to tear down fences, live again as a human being? Or has inhumanity built a fence that is unassailable – a fence that will allow no man to escape from torture even when bathed by time?

Each day I struggle to escape from this reality. Death, disease, diarrhoea; they stalk us. We waken, the weak January sun crawling slowly through the filthy glass, past the opaque frost crystals, to cast a blanket of despair across the dead and dying. Have no doubt, we are all dying here – except those who are already dead who have escaped their bondage in the darkness of the night. They have no need for fences now. Are they the lucky ones?

Those of us who struggle to sit upright, shake our dirty, shaven heads, slide from our bunks to the concrete floor below, prise our bodies into an upright position – or as near as beaten muscles will allow – shuffle to the door. What keeps us going lives in our imaginations on one side of the fence, the ability to sit in sunshine, watching fishes leap and fields turn golden. Without it we are no longer human. I thank God for my fence. Today the rumour is stronger: the Russians are coming.

Fate has decreed I live among the dead. I push a battered wooden trolley over chipped rails, a road to perdition. Or so it seems. For my cargo will be consigned to the flames on this man-made Hades. As the iron door shuts, the flames roar and another soul rises. Their fence has come down and there is the freedom of eternity.

As I trudge back along the track, my body and the trolley protest in unison, I hear a familiar screech. I do not look across for if I do, my fence will come down and I will face stark truth which I do not want. A train has halted, the cattle trucks clatter, buffer to buffer. The guards open the doors, shouting, 'Rouse, rouse.' I will meet most of this cargo as I wheel them to the ovens. But I stay on my side of the fence. My fence is high today. Listen brothers: the Russians are coming.

HERBIE BRIDGEMAN'S
HOLY WAR

It was raining again. It seemed to have rained all summer and now, as autumn neared, the showers were even heavier, at times torrential. The sky was leaden, the clouds were low; it was a miserable day. In the distance Herbert Bridgeman could hear the sporadic thunder of guns. He was getting closer. Then suddenly he was shaken from his thoughts as the Foden truck coughed and spluttered and lurched wildly to the right.

'Jesus Christ,' shouted Herbie, as he fought to keep the vehicle on the pitted, rutted and shell-pocked road and the engine running at the same time. He yanked desperately at the gear stick, his left foot furiously pumping the clutch as his right gently tickled the accelerator. The gears crashed noisily into place and the engine roared back to life once again. On each side of him was the grey, glutinous mud that could suck a soldier, unlucky enough to fall into it, to a slow and choking death. 'Christ,' muttered Herbie, 'what would it do to a lorry full of supplies?'

He shuddered and drove on.

Calm once again descended as he set his sights on the road ahead, the road to Ypres via Hell Fire corner. But he was – and not for the first time – disappointed in himself. Angry even. Taking the Lord's name in vain as he had just done twice in the space of a minute plunged him into a deep gloom that only caused his surroundings to darken more. He thought of his mother, a devout woman, and how disappointed she would be, for she had counselled him well over the years about the need to venerate the name of the Almighty. 'Ask for His help only in times of calm and not in moments of stress or in a voice filled with anger,' she had told him. Yet that is just what he had done – and not for the first time Herbie struggled to answer the question of why he did not share his mother's piety.

The guns were growing angrier now and he could see the smoke rising, hear the distant scream of shells and the crackle of gunfire. Or was it the screams of men dying and the sound of shattering bones? A cold chill ran down Herbie's spine. Here he was, bringing supplies of food and rum and ammunition for the brave men at the front and all he could think about was men dying. Perhaps that helped explain his lack of piety. 'If God is love,' Herbie mused, 'why has this become Hell on Earth?' His silent questioning of God's will dated from the time his father, a brave and experienced soldier, a good husband and kind father, had died, at the age of 39, from tuberculosis. It was at this point that the seven-year-old Herbie began to call God to account.

He could not, of course, ever discuss the matter with his mother. 'It is God's will,' she had told him. 'There is a purpose in all God does and it is not up to us mere mortals to question it.' Even at seven Herbie found this a weak explanation. What was God's purpose in taking a good man in his prime, a man who had served his country as a brave and loyal gunner, who had just left the army to take up the responsibility of providing a secure and loving home for his wife and son? And now, out there, He was again taking men often in agony and excruciating pain, for no real purpose.

Once again Herbie realised he was clutching the steering wheel with a manic intensity and, for a brief moment, allowed himself the thought that this might be God's throat. 'No, no,' he cried out loud, tears welling up behind his eyes. He touched his trouser pocket and felt the hard outline of the little metal crucifix his mother had given him before he left for France and peace returned to his mind.

Now he could see the flashes quite clearly and the sky began to darken even more; he must be nearing the line. Trees were shorn of their foliage and the road was even more pitted. Ahead a convoy of ambulances were coming towards him so he knew he was nearing the depot.

The ambulances had been busy since the Third Battle of Ypres began in June and Herbie knew that while substantial advances against the Hun were being achieved, it was at a terrible cost in life and limb. The weather had not helped and the fact that the delicate underground drainage systems, built over centuries by peasant farmers, had been smashed by the bombardments had turned the terrain into a treacherous sea of mud.

Hard as he tried, Herbie could not stop looking at the slow convoy as it passed him. 'Poor buggers,' he muttered. But then these were the lucky ones – or so it might be argued. Wounded brought back from the line were quickly assessed at the regimental aid post, while wounded who might live were patched up and sent further back to an advanced dressing station. Along the way soldiers, quickly examined by medical orderlies, whose hopes of survival were deemed limited, were made comfortable and left on stretchers to die. Those were army regulations after all.

For the soldiers in the ambulances the destination was the casualty clearing station some seven miles behind the line. Once you got to the hospital, well, the surgeon's saw quickly got started. Working under very difficult conditions, limbs were hacked off, bodies stitched up all on a near-industrial system. Doctors were frequently worked to exhaustion, standing in pools of congealing blood, so thick and sticky that, periodically, they had to be lifted out of their own boots that had become firmly stuck to the floor.

Herbie shuddered and for some unknown reason a picture of the plaster Madonna and child which hung in the parlour at home and which was much revered by his mother, flashed into his mind. He even recognised the tiny chip on the bottom left hand corner which had happened after it had mysteriously fallen from the wall immediately after his father's death and to this day sparkled like an eternal snow flake among the more sombre colours of the icon.

'Why,' he asked himself, 'why now?' He shook his head vigorously. The convoy of ambulances was slowly passing him away from the front.

'Poor sods,' he said out loud trying to focus his mind on what was going on around him. But Herbie was shaken – more shaken than he perhaps cared to admit. It was the picture of that bloody Madonna and child that had rattled him most.

Her passive yet smug face looking down at the innocent child in her arms giving hope to the world of a better . . . a better what? Pestilence? Disease? Starvation? Poverty? War? Destruction? Death? An agonising end on a muddy battlefield in Belgium of France?

'Bastard,' shouted Herbie. 'Bastard, bastard, bastard.' He was again clutching the steering wheel with a manic grip, plunging the Foden into deep puddles of grey mud as if by doing so he was smashing his mother's Madonna and child.

If there was a God, mused Herbie, why was this Hell on earth taking place? Whose side was He on? 'God is love,' his mother had said, 'He cares for all mankind in equal measure.' Yet in this stinking, rat-infested hole, where men of many nations were dying by the thousands every day, where was the equality of his love? 'We shall win this war because God is on our side,' the British and Dominion Expeditionary force commander-in-chief, no less a man than General Haig himself, had assured his troops. Herbie pulled himself back to reality; he was at the gates of the supply depot.

'You soldier – here, now,' the burley Sergeant was waving at Herbie. 'Quickly lad. I need you to go up the front.' Herbie was bemused. 'The lorry won't get to the front Sarg. No road. It would just . . .'

'I bloody well know that, laddie,' he snapped. 'You're going – in a ration party.

'But I'm a driver,' said Herbie. 'Don't ration parties come up from the troops in the line?'

'That's what should happen, laddie, but sometimes they get delayed and that's why I need you.' The very thought of going to the front line filled Herbie with dread. Too many of the boys with whom he had run as a lad had marched off enthusiastically to fight the Hun.

'You'll be back soon,' the recruiting Sergeant had said, as he welcomed them into Kitchener's New Army, 'and you'll be heroes. Think what the lassies will make of that. And what's more we'll keep you all in the same battalion. Lord Kitchener is very much of the belief that Pal's Battalions are the thing so you can fight alongside your mates.'

The idea, of course, had turned out to be a disaster. As young Tommies fell in the mud in battle after battle, often screaming in agony for their mothers, before succumbing to their wounds, the telegrams began pouring out from the War Office – frighteningly with so many of them addressed to neighbour after neighbour in the same street and district in town after town across the land.

'Shouldn't we wait a bit, you know, if they've just been held up,' offered Herbie hopefully. 'Aren't they out there somewhere?' The Sergeant pulled himself up to his full height. 'Oh yes, out there indeed.' Herbie noted the tinge or irony in the voice. 'Out there, yes. But not coming here or anywhere else for that matter unless of course, there is a heaven, in which case they'll be sitting at the Pearly Gates, poor buggers.'

'God is love...God is love...God is love,' his mother's voice was ringing in his ears and the world, briefly began to swim around him. The sergeant was speaking again . . . 'There are men dying out there for King and Country and the least we can do is make sure they get a hot meal and a good swig of rum before they go over the top. Now, get fell in with this ration party.'

The freshly promoted Corporal leading the party, a lad much the same age as Herbie, puffed himself up. 'Now don't ask me where we're goin' – 'cause I don't beedin' know,' he said pompously, pausing to laugh at his own humour. 'Well I do – but I don't if you know what I mean. See the line may have moved or the track is changed – or I simply get you lost.' He laughed again obviously enjoying his new-found power. 'Roight,' he said loudly, 'what we're gonna do is this. We pick up the containers, roight. Then youse follow me, roight. We goes down the duck boards as far as we can and then slip into the reserve trenches. We follows the communications trenches, roight, down through the other trenches until we reaches the front line and that's the job done. Roight.'

He smiled at the little group; he could sense the fear and that made him even more pompous. 'Just one or two little fings to remember,' a smile spread across his face. 'Don't wander off the duck boards or you're a dead 'un, roight, 'cause we ain't stopping to pull you from the bleedin' mud. Although it's dark, you can't show a light or a sniper will pick you off, roight. And for Gawd's sake don't light a fag, 'cause that gives our position away.' The Corporal waited for a moment relishing the gloom he had cast on Herbie and the others. Obviously saving the best for the last, he added: 'It bleedin' stinks out there. It's dead bodies, roight, decomposing. Sometimes they get so full of gas they actually explode. But don't worry, 'cause the rats get them. Bleedin' rats is feeding like lords out there and are as big as bleedin' cats, so make sure you don't add to their dinner, roight.'

The little party set off into the near total darkness, their way lit only by the scrap of moon which glittered on the raindrops and reflected in the shell holes in which dead bodies lurked. Slowly, step by step, and in total silence they made their way down the duck boards, the Dixies of stew carried on yolks across their shoulders much as a milkmaid might carry home through lush, sun-dappled, green pastures, the fresh, warm milk straight from the cow. However, unlike the milkmaid they were not skipping through the verdant green, but carefully picking their way along the slippery duck boards, every so often slipping dangerously close to the edge. Muttered curses hung heavily on the damp night air. 'For Christ's sake shut it,' said the Corporal in a loud whisper, 'or you'll have the whole bloody Hun army down on top of you.'

When Herbie awoke he focused first on the stars twinkling as they had done for ever and the partial moon across whose face clouds slowly drifted. He squinted for a moment to see if he could make out the face of the man in the moon who, as a child, he was assured was there. The silence, too, was refreshing. Not a sound could be heard. Stars, the moon and total peace – what more could a man desire? There was a certain warmth down Herbie's right side, rather like a giant hot water bottle had been laid there. Cautiously he felt with his hand and, yes, there was a soft warm . . .

'Christ,' shouted Herbie, 'it must be blood.' In fact, it was stew, fatty, warm and congealing that spilled from the Dixie as he and the others in the ration party had spun through the air with the greatest of ease to land in a shell hole as a fresh crater formed a few yards ahead of them and the blast propelled them through the evening air.

Herbie was conscious of movement beside him – and while he could hear nothing he realised that the Corporal was in deep pain. Having established that he, Herbie, could move without pain, he crawled to the lip of the crater. It was all peaceful now, no flashes of field artillery or streaks from snipers' rifles. Briefly he relished the total silence until it slowly dawned on him that he was now profoundly deaf. Herbie leaned back into the crater and gently pulled the Corporal's body towards him, noting the anguish on the man's face and the blood seeping from a chest wound. Gradually, and with not a little difficulty, Herbie manhandled the Corporal over his shoulder and, crawling in a crouched position, eased himself and his patient onto firmer ground. With great effort Herbie. the young Corporal slung across his shoulders and, half crouching, made his way slowly along the slippery duckboards. The sky lit up as a Very pistol propelled a phosphorous charge into the darkness and, seconds later, Herbie felt himself spinning round and round. This time he did not lose consciousness as it was bullets rather than shells that had ripped through the air. Herbie struggled from under the weight of the crumpled Corporal who now lay across him and as he sat up he realised the damp on his face was not perspiration, but the brains and blood of his dead comrade.

A shiver of revulsion ran through Herbie. What was God bloody well doing? Had He no compassion? How far did He think he could push Herbie and his fellow men? Scrambling to his feet, Herbie struggled to get the small crucifix from his pocket and, standing with his face to the night sky, roared: 'God! Where are you God? Show me your face.' He held his arm high and the crucifix glinted in the moonlight. 'God, God why do you persecute me?' he screamed. "Bastard, bastard, bastard." Suddenly the night sky lit up and Herbie realised that at last God might be going to speak to him and reveal why he had allowed Hell to be created on earth.

A hundred yards away, across no-man's land a German sniper carefully slid back the bolt on his rifle.

THE BETRAYAL OF LOYAL ROCHUS MISCH

The Russians are coming! Terror and fear are flowing through the corridors like a river in spate, swirling around me: loyal Rochus Misch - in the bunker designed by Speer, built by Hochtief AG of concrete and steel, below Berlin, for 1.35 million Reich marks, to hide the Fuhrer. *Heil Hitler!* Where is he anyway? No, not Speer – the Fuhrer? In his study planning the final assault. Good! He has a secret weapon to unleash, bringing final victory. Fantastic! The boys and the old men of the Volkssturmann are ready to fight at Potsdamer bridge until the Fuhrer unleashes the new weapon; saved at the eleventh hour! God bless the Fuhrer! He is our salvation. *Heil Hitler!* What? The Fuhrer has broken off his deliberations to marry Eva Braun? Why, that is good news. Bless them both!

Magda Goebbels passes. 'It will soon be over, Misch,' she says. She is grim of face. 'Yes,' I reply excitedly. 'The Fuhrer is planning the final assault and we have a secret weapon that will win the war.'

She does not reply and heads towards her children's bedroom. What is that small box she is carrying? It looks like medicine. I hope the little ones are not sick. My small switchboard springs into life. It is Jodl for Bormann, reporting from the front. 'It is not good news,' I overhear Jodl saying. Terror and fear once again; I am drowning. But are we not safe in the bunker; it will withstand everything and keep the Fuhrer safe. How did Speer know Berlin might one day fall? Steel and concrete. Impregnable. Deep down below Berlin. Shit, the Russians are pouring into Berlin, reports Jodl. I must stop listening in on these calls – they submerge me.

Achtung! Achtung! Fuhrer, unleash our secret weapon. NOW! Zhukov's army is on Potsdamerplatz.

The stores have been raided and those who have lost faith are drunk, hiding from reality. Surely Berlin will never fall? A Reich to last a thousand years the Fuhrer promised – he would not lie or deceive. Would he? Loyalty questioned. Disloyalty must be avoided. Drowning again. Should I join the revellers? No! I am loyal Rochus Misch. The Fuhrer needs me. He will ring through with orders to unleash the secret weapon - I must be here to connect that call. *Heil Hitler!* Then the war will be won. Trudl Jung has left the Fuhrer's study. So he is still giving her dictation; that is a good sign. 'Hi Trudl,' I call out. But she does not reply; she is crying. The Fuhrer must ring through soon with the order. *Achtung,* Fuhrer*! Achtung!* The Russians are here!

Dead! What do you mean? By his own hand? Impossible! Not the Fuhrer! And Magda's children! Oh God, not the little ones? Heavy artillery fire. Zhukov's thugs are on the steps of the Chancellery with a red flag, above the bunker. *Damn you Hitler!*

A VIEW FROM THE TRENCHES

In the early 1920s Private Tommy Atkins was asked by a local school about his memories of the Great War – the war to end all wars. This is an extract of that interview.

Tell us Tommy – What does war mean to you?
War is a hellish thing. War is a necessary thing. My war kept the world free – at least that's what they told us.

Why did you join up, Tommy?
I think it was early 1915. We were all pals, working together, gardeners you see, on a big estate. It was that night, in the pub, that somebody said, 'Let's fight for King and Country.' The next day we all signed up. Mad it seems now. But we did, and that was it. War called us, you see – or at least Lord Kitchener did for his New Army. He told us that if a gang of us signed up together we would stay together throughout the war. This was his Pals Battalions, you see. But the war destroyed us, if not in body then at least in mind.

When did you reach the front?
Well, we had basic training first. Christ it was tough. Mind you, I was used to hard work – but not to being bawled at all day long. We was looking forward to going to the front really. The idea of being heroes. We'd kill a few Huns, get some medals and the lassies back home would love us. At least that's what we thought.

Did it happen like that?
Bugger me; it was Hell, living Hell. Mud, you see – and rats. Rats as big as bloody cats 'cause they was living off the corpses of the dead. Bastards! I hate 'em. And the mud . . . friggin' mud.

Mile after bleeding mile of it. Flanders. Bloody Flanders. All that shelling had busted the drains the farmers had laid over hundreds of years and the good Lord, bless him, had decided to drop gallons of rain on us day after day. Mud! If you fell in that mate, you was done for. Your kit, you see, just pulled you down and the mud sucked you under faster than you could shout 'Help me mother!'

What happened while you were at the front?

Well, for days on end the Huns battered us with heavy artillery and then tried to storm our trenches. Then we'd batter them and try and take the trenches back. Trouble was barbed wire and machine guns. God, just the memory makes me shake. Then old General Haig, God bless 'im, well he had us cross the wire with 70lb packs on our backs walking in straight lines. The Hun just cut us to ribbons.

How did you survive Tommy?

A bloody big shell arrived in our trench one day and blew most of the lads to smithereens. When they dug us out I was still alive – just. It was a 'Blighty' for sure, hospital, then out. No more war for me. Well, I can't walk with only half a leg and I'm not much use with a rifle when I've only got one arm. But listen, mate, I was one of the lucky ones . . .

Tommy Atkins, thank you for talking to us.

A TALE FROM SHOE LANE

At the far end of Shoe Lane, in the village of Cobbler's End, there stands a house of some quality and substance called Leather Upper which was once owned and maintained by Lord Marmaduke Lacey's family. But it is the property further down the lane in which we are interested. It is a down at heel farm, called Lower Upper, where an old lady still farms sheep.

Although elderly and unkempt, she maintains a dignified pose although her pencil-thin fame is now supported by a walking stick. She is moving slowly, but with determination, to her farmhouse.

She is a widow, the wife of the Honourable Cosmo Lacey, second son of the family. He was disinherited several decades ago when he fell in love with a servant from below stairs. The family was horrified with Cosmo when he said he wished to marry the servant. No, no no, said the family in unison you cannot shoe-in upstairs that which belongs below stairs.

And so, it was that Cosmo and his new wife were given Lower Upper to enable them to keep body and soul together but also disinheriting him from any claims to the big house and lands. Sadly, Cosmo died early into the marriage from tuberculosis, leaving his young widow to tend their farm.

Time passed, agricultural practices changed, but life at Lower Upper remained mainly the same. Time walked steadfastly on but life at the farm did not follow. Although Cosmo had counselled his young wife to step into his shoes and progress life on the farm, at Lower Upper things had stood still.

Now pause for a moment and study the old lady – her clothes are shabby but clean – but her boots are covered in whatever they can collect while in a farming environment. They are wellington boots, for she eschewed wearing any other footwear except that which is on a shoe rack in the stone flagged kitchen, beside the old Aga: an elderly pair of brown brogues, in some need of shoe polish, that are kept for the rare special occasions when she needs to mix with the locals in the small village at the foot of the lane.

As she enters her kitchen she notices, to her displeasure, her two cats (elderly single ladies like to keep cats for companionship), are eating the last of the fish pie she was planning to heat up that evening on the rusting AGA.

'Shoo, shoo,' she cries as the mischievous cats scurry, 'shoo, shoo.'

THE MYTH-TERY OF MR BOND

The elderly civil servant looked hard at the young job applicant in front of him. 'Mmm,' he murmured as if deep in thought. 'Bond. James Bond. A name not unknown to me.'

'Yes,' replied the young man, a cheerful smile on his face, 'my grandfather. You know, 007, licensed to kill and all that.'

The elderly civil servant rubbed his chin thoughtfully before he spoke. 'Ah, the myth of 007. A piece of nonsense, I fear, Mr Bond.' The young man leaned forward a black look crossing his face. 'With respect sir, I think we may be talking at cross purposes?'

The older man sat back in his seat and sighed. 'No,' he said at last, 'we have the right James Bond.' There was another long silence. 'I suppose I'd better tell you the story as it was a long time ago, but you should be aware that this will destroy your grandfather's image. Shall I go on?'

'Of course,' the young man said. 'I think I have a right to know the truth. Give it to me plain and unvarnished.' The older man allowed himself a gentle smile. 'James Bond was a bounder and a cad, incompetent and dishonest. The department might well have covered it up had your grandfather not fallen in with that man Fleming in Jamaica. Indeed, had your grandfather not died he might have been prosecuted under the Official Secrets Act. Although my own view was there were no real grounds. But he was an embarrassment to the Service and the Government. There was a collective sigh of relief when he died.'

The young man looked crestfallen. 'But James Bond was a hero, one of M's top operatives and my grandmother was Miss Moneypenny, M's secretary. Is that not so?'

'I fear not young man. There never was an M. Your grandfather had an affair – one of many, I should add – with Effie McGuffie in the typing pool, a naïve girl from Slamannan. Your father was the result. The department quietly covered it all up and when the time came your father was sent as a boarder to Fettes College in Edinburgh.'

Ah,' cried the young man excitedly, 'grandfather's old school.' The aged civil servant looked at the ceiling for what seemed an age. 'Noooo. Your grandfather was quickly identified as intellectually and educationally sub normal. He went to Fountainbridge primary where they tholed him and later to Tynecastle from which he was expelled. He worked as a milk delivery boy for a time and then joined the navy . . .'

'. . . and rose to the rank of Commander,' said the young man eagerly. 'Not bad for a boy from a poor background.'

'Actually, he rose to the rank of Able Seaman and that only because of his intimate knowledge of brothels around the Mediterranean and his ability to source cheap alcohol during times of rationing. Somehow he was spotted by the department and in an action that was soon regretted, he joined us. This was largely because of his lack of education and sophistication so he could be passed off as a rough and ready type – eh, how can I put it? – from the labouring classes. This was useful when we were infiltrating spy networks as our enemies tended to ignore him. Your grandfather was very useful when it came to delivering packages and things like that because he was so – how can I put it he – he did not stand out in a crowd.

'The department made a fundamental error of judgement when we needed someone to be gambling in a casino where agents from the other side were known to be operating. It was known that your grandfather enjoyed gambling at which he had a great skill at cheating. His role for us was to be noisy and undisciplined at the tables and to draw attention to himself so that our senior agent could then have cause to strike up a conversation with the unwitting agents from the other lot.'

Later he was occasionally employed in gambling roles because of his life-long love of – eh, let me see, losing money at the tables and his enormous capacity for alcohol. All in all, it cost the department a lot of money. But we could not get rid of him just like that in case he began talking in public houses during his drinking bouts, particularly if he was in company with some of these distasteful people from Fleet Street.'

A thunderous look crossed the young man's face. 'No, no, this can't be the same person. My grandfather, the real James Bond, bankrupted Le Chiffre of SMERSH in the casino at Royale – he was a daredevil who saved this country from evil on many occasions and he died fighting a barracuda in the sea off Jamaica and . . .' His voice tailed off as he watched the elderly civil servant thumb through a dog-eared file.

'Alas, not so young man. Yes, your grandfather did play at Royale-les-Eaux but against a very minor SMERSH bodyguard – and lost. It was a considerable amount of the department's budget. He broke or lost more gadgets than the department could produce and caused more trouble during the cold war than we could cope with. He was eventually very generously pensioned off to Jamaica where he fell in with Fleming – a lethal combination as far as the department was concerned.'

The young man was crestfallen. 'So the family history is a complete load of bollocks?'

'Not quite,' replied the civil servant, 'he did die in Jamaica – but from cirrhosis of the liver, complicated by second degree syphilis. Now then, you are applying for a job in the department. Let me see, we have a post for a clerical officer in registry. No guns I'm afraid or licences to kill but you will get the opportunity to fight your way through mountains of paper.'

The young man rose from his seat and quietly left the room. 'Goodbye Mr Bond,' said the aged civil servant as he closed a file marked 'For M's Eyes Only.'

THE WAITING ROOM

The city is bustling, unlike the dining room in the private residential hotel. Here, in the Waiting Room, elderly residents in their twilight years, wait to meet God. They huddle round little stiff linen-covered tables sprouting, as if like summer daisies, from the brown carpet. It is the same ritual day-in day-out as they wait for God's call. There is a gentle hum; like summer bees seeking pollen. It is the whispered, sometimes conspiratorial, conversations of elderly residents. Two waitresses, one like a sparrow whose face maps a life of strife, the other a young woman built like a shire horse, move gingerly among the tables carrying meagre breakfasts; in the autumn of their lives the elderly eat little.

'That's a braw looking cup o' tea, lassie. Aye, in the cup. In the cup. Thank you kindly.' He wears a flat cap at all times; it matches the battered but once expensive tweed suit, that a long time ago fitted him like a glove but still, faded and jaded, still speaks of a comfortable bank balance. However, his hands as he reaches out to move his cup and saucer are large and damaged by years of toil. He has only recently moved to the Waiting Room.

Two tables away the Widow McCrindle and the Mistress Gellatly are huddled together; they whisper conspiratorially for they are refined Edinburgh ladies. The widow McCrindle has sold her flat in posh Morningside, paid off her late husband's gambling debts (of which she had no prior knowledge) leaving her, she hopes, enough to see her time out in the Waiting Room. Alas, Mistress Gellatly has not been so fortunate. A spinster from a comfortable but dated rented flat in Comely Bank where she had lived with her mother, she devoted her life to service in Jenner's fine store on Princess Street. Now she is trying to eke out her days on a meagre pension. Unlike Farmer's Hands whose total devotion over decades to growing broccoli, has left him by comparison, wealthy but lonely.

'It's disgusting,' says the Widow McCrindle, 'shouldn't be allowed in here, standards are falling. I don't know what my dear Herbert would make of it.'

'Indeed, indeed,' replies the Mistress Gellatly, 'he's farming stock, I think.'

'Rough country type, no refinements,' adds the Widow McCrindle.

'But healthy and wealthy,' sighs Mistress Gellatly. 'Never been married,' adding quickly, 'I'm not surprised.'

'You're not thinking . . .' mutters her companion aghast.

'Good heavens, NO! But there is a glint in the Mistress Gellatly's eye.

The Sparrow is moving between the tables, laying small brown envelopes in front of each guest as the Shire Horse begins the task of gathering in crockery and cutlery.

'Oh dear, our weekly bills. I do hope they haven't gone up again,' whispers the Mistress Gellatly.

Life for those who choose to end their days in private hotels in post-war Edinburgh carry with them a lifetime of experience and a considerable baggage of secrets. At precisely ten o'clock Farmer's Hands and Mistress Gellatly leave the hotel. Farmer's Hands crosses the road and soon boards a number 26 bus to Corstorphine, while Mistress Gellatly turns left and walks to the West End where she boards a number 17 bus which will allow here to alight at the entrance to the Western General Hospital.

Meanwhile the Widow McCrindle slowly climbs the stairs to her magnolia painted room. She is slightly breathless as she tussles with an important decision. She looks at her watch (a present from her late husband to mark their fiftieth wedding anniversary). She purses her lips; it is far too early in the day. But why not? One won't kill her, will it?

The number 26 bus has reached the centre of Corstorphine and Farmer's Hands alights. He follows the high stone wall outside Dr Cormack's house and his eyes light up as he sees the bright young face of a boy peering round the corner of the wall outside the public lavatory.

Miss Gellatly has a spring in her step as she walks back down the drive of the Western General Hospital after her oncology consultation. She has eschewed invasive treatment and knows how long she has with only a pain relieving drug. It is as if a weight has been lifted from her mind and means her meagre finances will allow her to see out her days at the private hotel. She makes a decision and chooses to take a number 19 bus to George Street and treat herself to coffee and a slice of cake at Mackie's in Princes Street. To hell with the cost: she is celebrating!

The Sparrow has hung up her apron and is now determinedly walking along Dalry Road to the tenement flat she shares with her husband, a disabled war veteran. She does not have a lot of time as she needs to be back at the hotel in time to clear up plates from the lunch time buffet. In the little time she has she will help her husband, now bed-ridden, with his toileting and make them both soup before she again has to scurry back to work.

Alas, when she reached their little flat The Sparrow finds her husband has soiled the bed and she requires to strip it, wash him down, heat some soup, fill a roll and then depart back to Haymarket and the Waiting Room. There is no time for her even to have a cup of tea and she hurries, nearly running along Dalry Road.

The Widow McCrindle is slouched back in the easy chair in her room an empty sherry bottle on the little table beside her. It is time for the buffet lunch and she is not sure she can navigate the stairs to the dining room. Recently she had a tumble on these stairs and she cannot repeat this or others may put two-and-two together and realise she is a secret drinker.

Unfortunately, the Widow McCrindle has another secret habit – she enjoys a periodic smoke and has lit up a cheroot and, feeling relaxed she gently closes her eyes, dropping the cheroot down the cushion of her chair.

Passing her door, the Shire Horse smells smoke and reaches for a nearby fire extinguisher. Alas, in her enthusiasm the extinguisher springs off the wall and the Shire Horse tumbles backwards down the stairs, breaking her neck. Other residents are aroused by the noise and an ambulance is called along with the fire brigade. It is quickly established that a second ambulance is requires as the Widow McCrindle needs hospital treatment for smoke inhalation.

A bus from Corstophine halts at Haymarket and Farmer's Hands alights, a look of pleasure on his face. He will now enter Ryrie's historic bar and have a pint and a whisky chaser before setting off for the buffet lunch in the Waiting Room. However, on leaving Ryrie's he has a heart attack (a minor one as it turns out) and collapses into the path of an on-coming bus. Luckily for Farmer's Hands the bus driver swerves and misses him – but ploughs into the small wall outside Haymarket Station. He too is being ferried across Edinburgh to the Royal Infirmary at Lauriston.

Breathless from hurrying The Sparrow exits from Dalry Road and is astonished at the scene that unfolds before her. But she has no time to stop and ask questions as the station clock tells her she only has two minutes before she is due back at work. Not that this matters too much – there will be no lunches served today. The Waiting Room is nearly empty.